Men in the Making

Men
in the
Making

STORIES

Bruce Machart

Houghton Mifflin Harcourt
BOSTON   NEW YORK
2011

www.hmhbooks.com

Library of Congress Cataloging-in-Publication Data
Machart, Bruce.
Men in the making : stories / Bruce Machart.
p. cm.
ISBN 978-0-15-603444-9
1. Men—Identity—Fiction. I. Title.
PS3613.A272525M46 2011
813'.6—dc22   2011009154

Book design by Brian Moore

Printed in the United States of America

DOC 10 9 8 7 6 5 4 3 2 1

for my father, and for my son

"Oh, don't you know?" She brought his hand gently up her hip and around to the flat of her abdomen, where she pressed it close again. "Don't you know? You're the most valuable and wonderful thing in the world. You're a man."

— RICHARD YATES, *Revolutionary Road*

CONTENTS

Men in the Making

Where You Begin

S AD TO SAY, but dogs get killed sometimes. Take a city like Houston, four million people and all those cars, sometimes it's bound to happen, but if you're like I used to be, it doesn't bother you so much. Anyway, before this is over there's one less dog in the world, so in case you're not like I was, fair warning.

But if you're like I used to be, when your fiancée of five months gets home from a day of slaving for that lawyer downtown, the guy who cuts her a check twice a month for the privilege of telling her what to do and watching her cleavage go red with splotches the way it does sometimes when she's flustered; when she makes it through the door and finds you scribbling your latest on a legal pad, still in your boxers with the newspaper untouched on the porch in its plastic wrap, the classifieds still tucked inside without a single job listing circled; and when a few minutes later she comes half naked and frowning into the hallway, as red-faced and eager for her evening shower as would be a farm wife after bleeding a hog, you know you're history.

Kaput. Finito. It's over and you don't even ask for that ring back. All you think is, Well, dip my dog, because that's a quarter-carat solitaire with not too damn bad color and clarity. Even so, you just let it go, chalk it up to a learning experience, like the time you bought a quarter ounce of oregano outside the Texaco station from a pock-faced Mexican kid with jeans about half fallen off his illegal brown ass. You chalk it up. You say, "That there's a loss." All it *can* be. Next time — smell the weed before you finish the deed, that's all.

But *this* time — this time, when Gloria Jean Thibedeux tells your worthless, workless leeching ass to hit the road and never even mind all that stuff about getting married, that's exactly what you do. You hit the road. You hit it with all the plop and flourish of a horse turd dropped from a disgruntled gelding on the downtown leg of the rodeo trail ride.

Of course, Gloria ain't making this easy. No, she's got to strip right down to nothing but pink satin and the soft white skin that's been penned up all day behind her *law-yer-want-some-coffee?* business suit, and when she tells you where to get off, it's suddenly clear that this here's no warning. Nope. Turns out you're on the receiving end of a full-blown pink slip, pink as those panties she's reaching back to pull out of her rear. Yes, sir, there she stands in some of God's finest creations: satin bikini bottoms and one of those clasp-in-front bras that even you can get right in the dark. Your Gloria, nothing else on but that ring you maxed out the plastic for, and for once you don't even think about the bills rolling in.

"Baby," she says, her hands perched on those breeder's hips you've thought at times might make any stints in the delivery room as easy as lying back for a nap on Sunday, "if you ain't landed a job out at one of them refineries to-day—that or sold one of your precious 'Drama in Real Life' stories to *Reader's Digest*—then it don't matter how it breaks my heart clean in two, you gonna need another place to stay tonight."

Nothing altogether new, of course. This ain't the first time. You've been warned before, maybe a dozen times over the past four months, and sure, you've been writing, but you've got thirty-three stories and so far not a single cash cow. And now—now there's no sense in begging, so you sit there for a while in the kitchenette, biding time with your elbows propped on the yellow Formica tabletop. The new story you've written—a real ringer about a retarded kid trapped underwater in an upside-down school bus at the bottom of a ravine—is almost finished, and guaranteed, you think, to bring home the cash money *Reader's Digest* is doling out for this stuff on a monthly basis. You watch Gloria's pale little hands and those wide-slung hips and somehow none of this surprises you—not the way she's staring, lips in a tight puckered O like you've farted and accidentally drawn mud in your drawers, not the way the a/c snaps to life in the attic and spills its cool rush of air into the room, not even the way four months back you lost your job at Exxon, where you'd spent three years loading fifty-five-gallon drums of Varsall into tractor trailers. Hell, not even the guilt-like squeeze in your conscience you'd felt growing steadily tighter when, to pay your share of this month's rent, you sold the old El Camino you'd had since high school. Anymore, nothing's a surprise, but they say the expected ain't always easy, and now there's that slow grandfather clock of a feeling you get in your guts, like your heart's swinging way too low on a thin wet string in the wide-open empty insides of you.

"You best snap out of it," Gloria says, flipping that long black hair over her shoulder, and you can't help thinking it—*looks like a horse's tail swatting flies.* "I'm serious as murder one," she says. "Piddle-farting around in your underpants. Home all day writing your little stories. Out with Jimmy two nights already this week doing God knows what. Sweet Jesus, legal pads stacked up everywhere. You can't even clean up after yourself, let alone scrub a toilet or do a load of laundry. Let *alone* take care of a wife.

"You better *go*," she says, crossing her arms over the mess of red splotches on her chest. "For good. Right goddamn now."

Still you're waiting, leaning on the table like it needs holding down and waiting until it comes, the end-all to your be-all: "Toot sweet," she says, the thoroughbred Cajun twang alive in her voice, and you reckon that's all she wrote, so there ain't nothing left but to call your pal Jimmy

Love, tell him to come do his duty as your only real friend, former coworker, and owner of the '92 Chevy truck that's seen you riding shotgun while drinking off no less than three major league cases of what Jimmy always calls the post-poon blues.

What happens next, you might say, is about as predictable and necessary as a toothpick after corn on the cob. There's your father's old army duffel bag on the street beside you and you're kicking the curb, flipping pages of your legal pad when Jimmy Love comes rumbling up. Reaching over, he swings the passenger door open and pulls the hairs of his mustache down over his lips with a cupped hand.

"Well," Jimmy says, "don't know about you, but I'm picking me up a little hint of that déjà vu," and when you toss the duffel into the back and climb in he pats the two six-packs beside him as if they're the fair-haired heads of sons who just caught a greased pig at the state fair. "This make four?" he says. "*Damn.* Four women? In two years? And your sorry ass actually wanted to *marry* this one? Level with me, man. You having problems getting it up?"

Jimmy can be like this, all that sprawl-on-the-couch-and-tell-me-all-about-it bullshit. "Just drive," you say, slamming the door, because you get it up just fine, and besides, the details ain't none of his business. "Do the loop."

It's not something that needs saying, of course. All the elements are in place. Jimmy's behind the wheel, steering that old truck out of Gloria's rent-house neighborhood and up onto Highway 225 where the stainless pipes of refineries and chemical plants wind and shine under the evening's last dose of sun. With the black spill of their smokestacks, you'd swear they were bent on hurrying the night along. As for Jimmy, he drives with the Southwestern Bell Yellow Pages balanced on his lap, and when he accelerates over the ship channel, there's Loop 610, thirty-eight miles of five-lane highway that never ends but just keeps circling the Houston skyline from six or so miles out.

"We're on," Jimmy says, merging into traffic behind a dump truck with them Haulin' Ass babes on the mudflaps, and when he gets the phone book balanced on the gas pedal and checks the speedometer, he goes, "The Ma Bell cruise control's a go, you homewrecker. Let's drink."

You crack the window and out come the beers. The whole town smells flammable. "Yeah, keep talking," you say. "But I don't exactly see you settling down."

"Nope," he says. "Don't see me buying diamonds every time some coon-ass gets my dick hard neither." He swigs his beer and hits the wiper/washer. "Me and this Chevy, we can flat squash some bugs, ain't it?"

When you don't answer he pulls on his mustache and makes a clicking sound with his tongue. "Come on, now," he says. "You know me, I didn't mean nothin' by it."

You know Jimmy, all right. Here's a guy with—as he'll tell you—*a truck and some luck and on good nights a fuck.* A guy just far enough out of his mind to own the Exxon shipping and receiving record for blindfolded forklift driving—all hundred and five feet of the loading dock and down the ramp without ever putting on the brakes. Yup, Jimmy's got more bowling shirts than sense, but you've been knowing him a long time, and when tit turns to trouble he ain't ever late in that truck. He's good people, Jimmy, never mind all his ribbing.

"Don't go to fidgeting," he says. "Relax and drink your beer."

You do, and it's not as cold as it could be, but it slides down just fine so you take all twelve ounces in one pull and watch the Texas flag flapping on the can as you crumple it with one hand. Yup, still Lone Star, because it don't matter that some pantywaist snow bunnies from up north own the brewery now—it's still made in Texas and you'd just as soon raise your voice in the Alamo shrine as drink some mule piss from Milwaukee. Gloria, you know, is wrapped in a towel a few miles back, and the can in your hand can't help but remind you of the dark beer she buys by the case. "Blackened Voodoo," she'd said, "from N'Orleans," and when she poured some into your bellybutton once, it set you to tingling from shin bones to shoulder blades. It was one of the first nights, when the sheets were all crumpled up on the floor and she sat upright atop you, your legs pinned beneath those hips. And before she slurped the beer from you, she reached down, easing you inside of her, and while she rose and fell, tightening those magic muscles around you, you'd caught yourself thinking some pretty silly goddamn things—something about love, *love* for chrissakes, and how you might could get used to this. About how, when she lowered herself down on you, she made a little piece of you disappear in such a slow and painless way you didn't care if she ever gave it back. About how, because of that pool of dark beer in your navel, you couldn't see down to where way back yonder something had stopped and you'd begun.

"Time for numero dos," Jimmy says now, crumpling his first can.

It's practically instinct. Loop 610, thirty-eight miles round trip, six beers apiece. With the evening traffic thinning out, get that phone book just right on the gas pedal and you can figure on a steady seventy mph. Do the math, you get five and a half minutes per beer and, by God, if all's in your favor you'll still be thirsty when you make it back round to the ship channel. Then there's no telling, maybe a night at Frogs, the bar where the Exxon boys go after the second shift, maybe nothing more than twelve more beers and another half hour driving the loop.

"You still ain't given me the skinny," Jimmy says, wincing back the first sip of his new beer. "Was it the work thing again? 'Cause you ain't found a job?" Checking the rearview, he steers past a rusted tanker truck and all eighteen wheels are screaming to beat all, so he takes a swig and waits, smiling at you like maybe you're a sweet young thing he's grown suddenly fond of. "Go on," he says. "Ain't nothin' to be ashamed of, got dumped is all. Happens."

You're thinking, *You bet. Real deep, Jimmy.* But you know there ain't nothing to say. Should have looked for work today instead of doing all that scribbling. But goddammit, you think, this is some kind of story and she was getting a little uppity anyhow and then, well—*then* you're off to the races.

"I'm-a tell you what, Jimmy, this one's for real. This story, the one I'm writing today? Got this bus driver in it, and he been known to tilt a few back, you know? Well, kids ain't stupid so they take to calling him Boozer, right? And Boozer's first and last stop—this is down in the Valley, you know, long-ass bus rides down there—and anyway Boozer's first and last stop is this retarded kid. Small town, they ain't got one of them short little buses, you know? Them tard buses?"

A little chuckle from Jimmy now, and you know you've got him.

"So, Boozer likes this kid, right? Feels sorry for him and all, but he's a stomp down, pure-D-fucking miserable drunk, and he's already been about waist deep in the bottle the day it happens. What happens is this—got this part from the news last night—Boozer's looking back at this retarded kid while he heads out toward the ravine, making sure the other kids ain't picking on him and the like. He's cruising this long stretch of highway out west of Harlingen, nothing but caliche and sod farms, and he keeps checking the rearview, looking after the kid when Wham!, there's this horn and old Boozer's way over into the wrong lane with this gravel truck about to drive right down his throat. And then—"

"Then he jerks the wheel," Jimmy says, swirling his beer, "and all them poor little bastards break through the guardrail." He takes a swig and smacks his lips. "And off they go into the ravine and end up breaking their necks or getting knocked silly and drowning themselves."

Jimmy moves into the right-hand lane around, best I can tell, about twenty-five Mexican folk, so help me God, in one old beat-to-shit Ford Tempo. "Must be going to Walmart," he says, pulling on his beer.

You go, "How'd you know?" and he looks at you like all of a sudden maybe you're not answering to your own name.

"Where else?" he says. "Been to Walmart lately? It's all Mexicans. You'd think piñatas was on sale permanent."

"Jesus, Jimmy," you say. "About the bus, how'd you know about the bus?"

"Like you said, man. TV news."

It smarts a little, this guy busting into your story when he's supposed to be listening. "Yeah," you say, "but in *my* story the retarded kid lives. Sure, he's pinned underwater awhile and Boozer's about ten sheets to the wind, but that's why it's drama, man. 'Cause Boozer keeps diving after the kid, just keeps diving and diving, coming up for air, and he can see the kid down there, alive and wide-eyed and pinned beneath one of those bus seats that's come loose in the crash. Old Boozer's gasping for breath, spitting water, but he ain't giving up. He keeps going down, diving again and again as the bus fills up higher with brown water, and the whole time his head's just swimming with a three o'clock drunk. He's maybe fucked up royal, but you better believe he's gonna save his little friend."

Now Jimmy takes the phone book off the gas and puts his foot down hard. "But that ain't real life," he says. "No one lived, you saw the news. Facts is facts. That's what your folks at *Reader's Digest* is after. 'Drama in *Real* Life,' get it?"

That's when it happens. You see it coming out the corner of your eye. Just as Jimmy looks down to get another beer, something dark and fast flashes across the on-ramp ahead, then another something darts across, this one bigger, and by the time Jimmy pulls his head out of his ass you're bracing yourself—elbows locked—while the truck rears back and the tires smoke and Jimmy's standing on the brake. And then that sound comes. Not the squeal of the brakes, not the smack of that big black dog against the grill of the truck. Hell with that, you don't even hear that stuff. No, sir, if you're like I was, what you hear is the man screaming from the side of the highway, *No!* and *God No!* and *Oh no!* over and over while the dog slides away from you on its back, its thick black fur peeling on the concrete, rolling up like wet carpet under the poor damn thing while it slides and slides and keeps on sliding. And then Jimmy's got the truck over to the shoulder and he's throwing empties under the seat, saying, *Holy shit* and *Stupid dog* and *Great goddamn* while you're zeroed in on the man who's walking toward you now with his face—no shit—actually buried in his hands, and you start to put the pieces together.

There's the guy's truck on the feeder, all jacked up with its hazards on and a tire leaning against the rear bumper, and then there's the dog, now still and limp and backing up traffic and not even alive enough to regret chasing whatever it was that must've caught its eye.

"*Yow*," Jimmy says. "You all right?"

You and Jimmy been friends a long time, but still you tell him to *shut up*, just *shut the fuck up*, because there's this man coming up to the truck, and it don't matter at all what else is real or fake. Because it don't matter if he's got a wife or kids or a fiancée that's given him the boot or nothing. *Shut up*, you say, with a hand on Jimmy's chest, because outside that man is stopped now and kneeling on the asphalt shoulder and there's nothing else to say but that he's coming undone on the side of the road, crying for a dog he loved a whole damn lot, and well, when it comes right down to it, if you're like I was you've never felt like that, and all you know is that the whole thing makes it feel like that little heart has quit swinging inside you—only you don't know how, because you feel all tore open and exposed to the elements and there's traffic blowing by like mad and wind pushing in the windows thick and fast, the way that brown water must've poured in on Boozer, and the sound it makes is all muddled and crazy and broken to bits like the prayer you can't quite piece together inside you, the one that says, *Please God, someday, let me have that much to lose*.

The Last One Left in Arkansas

I'M NO ARKANSAS native. Still, I've seen my share of strange skies. After Anne and I were married, we left Texas so that I could attend forestry school in Oregon. From the balcony of our apartment just south of Eugene, we'd watch the black Pacific clouds roll into the Willamette Valley and even the birds would go quiet. It was a West Coast thing, like an earthquake—eerie, breathtaking, sometimes terrifying, but usually short-lived—over before the real panic had time to set in. When I was a kid in the Texas panhandle, clouds were recreation. God's truth, early one September the entire third grade skipped the afternoon half of school to follow a low nimbus across the scrub-grass field toward the creek bed. It was recess. Someone started walking and we all followed, cooling ourselves under the only outdoor shade we'd seen in months.

That was Texas. This is Arkansas.

Here in this valley, clear through to March, when on nights like tonight I sometimes sit on the porch in my parka, sipping whiskey and shivering and trying to find just the right prayer for the son I lost eleven years back, or the courage to call the one who's alive but living hundreds of miles away, often even the clouds turn lethargic, and they sit, and they stay.

They stay in such a way that tonight, if you sat in your truck at the intersection of the mill road and Highway 10, where the company land ends and the Ozark National Forest stands like a frozen wall to the north, your wipers would groan as they raked sleet from the glass. The clouds would hunker down, blocking out the moon, but even with one headlight out you'd be sure to notice that they haven't replaced the sign on the corner yet—it still reads 329 DAYS WITHOUT AN LTA. Lost time accident, that's what they call it when someone saws through an arm or shears a hand in half with the planer. All it takes is a second of distraction, one turn of the head. One bad decision. When you spend a quarter of your life in the mill, you have to remember every second what the motors and blades are capable of. You don't wear loose-fitting clothes and you don't take a drink at lunch. You don't work at a station before you've been trained and certified. When you're on the line, you don't think about your wife's nice plump ass and you don't worry about little Johnny's grades. You concentrate. I did it for ten years before I made plant manager, still do it when I'm out in the yard. There's rules and, as they say, you follow them so you can clock out and make your way home to play "This Little Piggy" with your babies without coming up short any piggies.

Something else you don't do—you don't clear sap build-up from between a pulley and belt when the conveyor is running. I've seen it tried and there's only one possible outcome: the belt doesn't slip and the pulley won't stop and the pillowblock bearings won't let loose of the shaft. It's one shoulder socket versus a forty-horse motor and the arm is coming off. Period. Every time. No question and no excuse.

I didn't know this Lonnie Neiman well, but I know what he didn't know. There's only one way to clean the debarker. That thing's a bad SOB, a real widowmaker, and you've got to respect it. You disconnect the power line. You call the electrician and have him cut the juice completely. It's something you'd expect everyone would know, but you've got to watch the new guys. They'll sweat their rears off, they'll *yessir* and *nosir* you to death, but when it comes down to it, they're just too damn eager, too revved up to slow down and think. The boys say Lonnie was like that, a whole mound of red ants in his pants. It's hard to believe, such a lack of common sense, such outright stupidity, but you can't tell his mother that. You can't say, *I'm sorry something awful, ma'am, but the boy was just too dumb to stay alive.* You can't even say for certain what the hell he was doing in there, except you have to figure that, with a kid like Lonnie, less than a year out of Blue Mountain High and just three weeks on the job, he was probably trying to go the proverbial extra mile, trying to make an impression. Well, if you ask my line foreman, Big Red, the kid did just that.

So did the debarker.

Imagine a porcupine turned inside out, a big mother with three-foot-long steel quills. That's what a debarking drum is like. An enormous pipe, fifteen feet in diameter and lined inside with hundreds of these quills. Load it with a dozen or so twenty-foot-tall, forty-year-old Arkansas pine trunks, turn that sucker on, get it rolling good, and thirty seconds later you've got naked trees, fresh and clean as an Eden stream. Step back, blow the bark and sap out the discharge vents, smell that rich, sappy-sweet smell, and keep on keepin' on. Now, load that killer with one six-foot-tall eighteen-year-old kid. Let's say he's a real green-ass, maybe he's trying to suck up to the foreman, do some extra housekeeping before the shift ends—who knows? All the same, he's in there when Big Red throws the switch to cycle the motor.

Red's been a crew chief for seven years, and if Red says there wasn't any screaming I've got to believe him. Just a bump, he said, a liquid whistling sound. Something that didn't ring right in his ears—that debarker is Red's baby and he would know. Then he opens the discharge vents and a few minutes later the boys find him puking his guts up in the washroom.

That was three days ago. Tonight it's history, the sign by the highway just doesn't tell the story yet. 329 DAYS, it reads, WITHOUT AN LTA, like maybe Rita in the front office couldn't stand to pull the numbers off the board and hang a zero in their place.

Usually, when I leave the sawmill for the night, I roll the truck windows down and breathe in deep through my nose. I take some of it home that way, some of the smell, some of the life that even a felled tree keeps holed up inside. It means something to me, makes clear the persistence, or maybe resistance, of the organic. Something dies—even a tree—it rarely goes willingly. It wants you to smell what it was in life, or what it could have been if you'd had the sense to let it go on living. It wants you to remember. Trees, like angry husbands and wives, always want the last word.

When I was ten, my father held me in front of him at Uncle Weldon's processing house in Odessa. After Dad had me choose the calf, my cousin Frank loaded a bullet into a special sledgehammer, and when he swung there was a dead, dull sound—no resonance—like maybe he'd dropped a wrecking ball into quicksand. Later, with the calf hanging from a hook inside, my uncle pulled a knife up through the smooth hide of the animal's underside and stepped back as the bulge of intestines slumped forward with a sucking sound and plopped onto the slick cement floor. What I remember most was Dad's breathing, the way his chapped lips clamped shut below his wiry mustache, the way his nostrils flared as he inhaled, sucking the smell of the animal into his lungs, keeping it alive awhile longer inside him.

Usually, for me, it's the same with trees, but lately it doesn't matter. The rain is freezing in midair and the stripped logs in the mill yard are sealed with skins of ice. It's winter in Logan County, Arkansas, and you can't smell a damn thing.

This evening, before Red and I took care of the smell in the debarking drum, on my way to Lonnie's wake the clouds were gray slate, perfectly smooth, spitting pebbles of sleet down on the countryside. The trees beside the road stood coated with ice, polished skeletons with bark-brown marrow. My driver's side headlight has been out for a week, and the dark and the ice on the road and the thought of coming face-to-face with Lonnie's mother were all mixed up like frozen slush in my gut.

Dangerous as it was, I stomped on the gas and rolled the windows down, and for the ten-mile stretch of highway I sped cold and half blind and sliding through turns toward town. I told myself that I just wanted it done, that I'd make my appearance at Wickman's Funeral Home and get it over with so I could head to my house and pour a whiskey and have a seat on the back porch. But what I really wanted, I suppose, was what I've wanted all winter—to be normal, a forty-seven-year-old lumber boss with a son gone off to college in Texas and an ex-wife who runs a nursery in Abilene. To forget about this poor kid who got himself killed in my debarking machine. I wanted the clouds to clear so I could sit in the sun on top of Magazine Mountain. I wanted my oldest boy back, wanted him alive. And I wanted like hell to smell the sticky insides of trees.

Now, if you were there in that truck near the edge of town, with sleet stinging your face and the highway ice slapping against the fender wells, and you decided you'd had enough of this maniac driver you'd somehow become and did what I was tempted each mile to do — that is, turn the truck around and let Lonnie's family and friends tend to his wake — you'd drive five miles west, just shy of half-way back to the mill on Highway 10, and then, near the foot of the mountain, on the other side of the road near a stand of pin oaks, you'd slow down, hang a right just after the yellow mailbox. From that point on, you could put it in neutral and coast all the way to the barn, half a mile, the grade just steep enough to pull you home, gravel dredged from the Petit Jean River crunching under your tires the entire way, and when a few hours later, after Lonnie's wake and after a trip to the mill with Red, I made it home to join you on the porch for a drink, I'd give you the nickel tour and tell you how the place used to be a farm. Chickens and pigs mostly, and corn.

I'd say that the old boy who sold it to me kept rambling on about the soil. "Uncommon dark for these parts," he'd said, spitting tobacco through the gap of his teeth. So proud, he seemed, and sad to be selling, that I didn't have the heart to tell him I hadn't planned on farming. I'd just wanted a quiet place set back away from the highway, but my wife, Anne, she must have been listening to him, because before I got a fresh coat of paint on the place, she'd tilled up a patch of ground between the barn and the back porch.

The daughter of a toolpusher from Abilene, and the only sister of four older brothers, Anne was always at home in a world ruled by muscle and force. Lean and strong, she was a physical woman, forever in touch with her body, and luckily, I always thought, remarkably in touch with mine. She called making love "roughhousing," and at times, especially early in our marriage, that seemed like an understatement. When angered, she was more likely to elbow you in the chest or smack you atop the head than resort to the silent treatment. She was a woman who spanked her children as soundly and shamelessly as she hugged them, who swung a hoe hard and took pride in her work, all the while wearing a dress. I can't do it justice, I'm sure, but watching her at work in that garden, or driving nails into the side of the barn so she could hang her tools there, her calves taut and shining in the evening's last hint of sun—well, let's just say it made me do math. In my head. *How many steps between us? How long to close the gap? How many seconds to get her up the stairs and out of that dress? How long could I keep her there beneath me? How long could I keep her?*

Just the thought of that garden, I admit, fills me with something crackling and sharp, an electric kind of longing. It was quite a sight, something to come home to, something alive and green and ever-changing, especially in springtime when the sun was still out. I'd roll up in my old truck, beat down and dusty from a day at the mill, and

Anne would be squatting in her garden in one of those short, flowery dresses, her toes curled up in the earth, the roots of her long blond hair darkened with sweat. She'd spend hours out there babying those plants. So many that I used to tease her, claiming she loved them as much as she loved the boys, and for years after she left I thought for sure it was true, but that was anger talking, the kind that's sometimes long-lived and almost always laced with self-pity. The kind that finds a man sitting nights on his porch in the dead of winter, sipping whiskey, wondering why he's alone, the only one still living his life, the last one left in Arkansas.

Some nights, if the whiskey can't find its way into my glass, and I can keep myself off that back porch and out of sight of where Anne's garden used to be, when I think about her I can admit to myself that she loved our boys as much as any mother, and that, sure, she loved her garden, and that it doesn't make any sense to compare the two. Lose a plant and you learn to respect the elements, to prepare for them. There's no one to blame but yourself. Lose a child and, for a while, the only thing that can keep you sane and above ground and alive enough to hate yourself is the burn-off of rage you ignite by laying blame somewhere, on something or someone else, so you can keep it from burrowing inside you and living where deep down you believe it belongs.

Plants and children.

I was acting the fool to ever compare them, or to think that Anne ever had, but what I do accept is that all her af-

fections grew from the same source. It was the raising she
loved, the cause and effect of nurture and growth. When
our firstborn, Nate, started walking, she tacked a cloth tape
to the inside wall of our closet and measured his progress
against the pencil marks she made on the wall. I remember
his laughter, so high and happy, at being tucked away in
that closed quiet space with his mother, the woman who
cooed and praised him for every half inch.

I remember Anne's routine before she was pregnant
with our second boy, Matty. She'd groan when I got out
of bed and dragged myself to the shower, but by the time
I'd dressed she'd have Nate's food warming in a sauce-
pan and mine sizzling on the griddle. When I'd leave for
work, she'd be weeding in the garden, telling little stories
to Nate, who'd be sitting in a white diaper between two
rows of carrots. When I got home at night, the place would
hold signs that life had gone on inside—dishes from lunch
stacked in the sink, wash going in the utility room—but
she'd usually be back in the garden, sometimes weeding,
mostly watering. Always talking. She spoke to them—her
son, her plants—as if they were somehow interchangeable.
"A little water for you," she'd say, and then she'd turn the
hose to Nate's feet, and he'd laugh and flap his arms and
wiggle his toes while Anne said, "and a sprinkle for you, big
boy. Just look how big we're all getting."

Her plants and her son. They grew up together, heard
the same encouraging words whispered, rooted in those
same rows of soil. Then Anne started growing, and by the

time Matty came into our world, the garden was four years in the making, the same age as Nate.

Anne had a knack for knowing things early. She could tell by nightfall whether the next day would bring rain—said she could hear it in the wind, that it sounded like a seashell tide—and her garden was rarely overwatered. In the spring, she never brushed the soil back from the tops of the carrots. She knew by the shape of the greens how long to wait. And two months before he was born, Anne knew something was wrong with Matty.

"It's not right," she said one night, climbing into bed. "It feels like everything's all mixed up inside."

She brushed her thumb over my lips and her face folded into furrows. With my finger, I traced the darkening line that ran from her distended belly button to her panty line. "We've seen the ultrasound," I said. "Doctor says everything looks fine."

"I know, Tom." Her eyes were wide. She took hold of my ears and leaned in close. "But I feel it," she whispered, "and it's all wrong."

Looking back, and knowing how this has all turned out—with her in Abilene and me still out here in the valley alone—it might sound naive, but I was a man who trusted his wife. I believed in her body's warnings the way I believe a green sky during tornado season, so when nine weeks later I was called from the waiting room and found

Anne upright in bed, holding our baby to her breast, such
a charge of relief rolled through me that I took hold of the
bed railing to keep my balance. I must have been grinning
to beat all, and Anne smiled too. A slight, exhausted smile.
Her hair hung in wet, matted ropes at her neck and tiny
beads of sweat clung to her forehead. She pulled back the
blanket and there he was, our Matty, sleeping and sucking
softly. Anne looked up at me, then her eyes dropped down
to her child and she pressed her lips so tightly together
that her chin began to quiver. Pulling the blanket back fur-
ther, she uncovered Matty's twisted foot. It was tiny, pink,
dimpled like a new potato, and I remember tilting my head
like a puzzled dog, thinking it might all make sense if I
could just get the right perspective, but it was no use. I
leaned closer, praying I'd find toes, and I must have looked
ridiculous, a grown man all twisted up around himself, so
obviously keeping his distance from the freak object of his
curiosity. A man frightened by his own son, afraid to hold
the tiny foot in his palm and raise it to his cheek, or warm
it with his breath.

Anne didn't look up at me. She kept her eyes down and
stroked Matty's head with the backs of her fingers. I don't
know how long I stood there, but I remember wanting the
comfort of Anne's eyes on me, wanting her to know we'd
be okay the way she knew about the weather, wanting her
to know it so surely that I would too. But more than that, I
wanted her to share the awkward silence somehow, even if
her look was unknowing, or piercing, or fierce.

I must have sat there for an hour, maybe longer, a solid

block of fear in my stomach. And when I left the hospital, carrying a nauseating uncertainty out to my truck with me, I didn't know what to do next. Before that day and since, I've heard parents tell guilt-riddled stories about forgetting their children—maybe starting the car and backing onto High Street before realizing the baby's still sitting in his stroller on the sidewalk, being an hour late to pick a child up after Little League, that sort of thing—and all I can say is that sometimes, no matter how long they've been toddling underfoot, you surface from somewhere in the undertow of your thoughts to the sudden and crashing realization that you're a parent. That afternoon, I must have driven the back roads for half an hour, and only after gunning the engine on the downhill stretch of Highway 10 and circling around our land on the gravel farm road did I remember Nate. I veered off at the fork and headed toward our neighbor Mrs. Janson's place, where I'd left him that morning.

I found Nate out back, perched on the iron seat of an antique tractor. His hands gripped the wheel and his head was thrown back, his lips sputtering with the sounds of imaginary harvest.

"You've got a brother," I told him, wiping some of his engine slobber from the corner of his mouth. "A baby brother."

His eyes focused in on me with a serious precision that looked artificial on the face of a child. "Okay, Daddy," he said, raising his arms to be picked up. "Let's go see."

It's unsettling sometimes, how the roles of father and

son get jumbled, how much security a four-year-old can offer a man, but Nate's raised arms and the matter-of-fact look on his face set me at ease, and I remember actually whistling while driving us back to town.

"Mommy," Nate said when we came into the room. "Is that one ours?"

Anne nodded. "Come see," she whispered, pulling back the blanket.

Matty was sleeping and dreaming and sucking at air. Nate pressed his palms to the new pink skin of his brother's chest, and something about the solemn and gentle look on his face reminded me of a holy man, a preacher, and as Nate laid hands on Matty his lips moved with half-whispered thoughts that resembled prayer. He froze when he saw the foot, but one look at his mother and her smiling nod was all the reassurance he needed. He took Matty's shriveled foot in his little brown hands and held on to it.

Anne raised her eyebrows and winked at me. She held out her hand, the corners of her lips curled into a sad smile, and when I went to her I realized that I'd come for them all. I couldn't wait to carry them home, all three of them, to pile them into the truck and drive them out of town, back down the hill through the shadow of the mountain and into our valley.

From that first day, Nate took possession of his brother, and when Matty turned two, Nate decided that he should walk. Nate stood facing his baby brother and pulled him up by the arms, holding him steady while Matty forced his first uneven steps toward the encouraging face of his teacher. For Nate, this was serious business, and Matty walked. Two years later, when the mill's insurance finally agreed to pay for prosthetics, Matty followed Nate everywhere, even into the bathroom. He'd walk slowly, his arms tense at his sides, his face scrunched up like he'd licked a lime.

"What's wrong with him?" I said. "He need to go number two or something?"

Anne laughed and rolled her eyes. "He's trying to walk like Nate," she said. I turned to watch him creeping behind his brother into the kitchen. "Without the limp."

Nate was determined that Matty be normal; looking the part was never enough. The first day of second grade, Matty cried out from the boys' bedroom that he couldn't find his arm braces. By that time he was walking fine without them, only a slight limp, but he tired easily. He'd already made a habit of spending hours alone, playing quietly indoors or reading in his room, and he grew more impatient and irritable the longer he was on his feet.

"I'll help him," Nate said, now a cool, burr-headed sixth-grader, and minutes later they emerged from the back hall together, Nate with a hand on Matty's shoulder. Anne was flipping pancakes onto plates, we all sat down to breakfast, and later Matty walked to school without his braces, his older brother at his side.

This past August, while Matty was packing his things for his move to college, I did some rooting around in the attic. I was digging through a hope chest, trying to find the brass cigarette lighter my grandfather had gotten as standard issue while serving in World War I. He'd given it to my father, who gave it to me, and even though my son and I don't smoke, it was the only family heirloom I'd ever had, and I wanted to press it into Matty's palm before he left me for college. Crawling out of the attic, I saw one of Matty's old braces sticking out of a box, and I took it down with the lighter.

"You remember the day you quit using these?" I asked, and Matty smiled, his eyes bright.

"You mean the day Nate hid them from me?" Matty said. He raised his eyebrows and nodded at the old lighter in my hands. "What else you got there?"

In the years since Nate's death, nothing I asked of Matty had come free of charge. A few days after the funeral, I'd sat the boy down and pressed him for details about the accident. I wanted to know if he'd seen Nate after the crash, if my oldest had moved, or spoken, or if Matty had seen him breathing. Anything. But Matty just sat there, his fingers drumming the kitchen table. "I'm hungry," he said, so I took him to town and bought us a pizza. A small gesture, I thought. Hardly a bribe. His favorite dinner for an hour of conversation. At first, I thought it a harmless exercise. After all, Matty had shared a bedroom with Nate, had walked to the bus stop with him on school days, had seen him and talked with him and laughed and joked with him for hours each day while I tended to business at the mill. I couldn't help myself. I wanted these stories. I wanted the time I had missed, and over the years I found myself engaging in all kinds of bargains, buying Matty's memories of his brother. Paying for bits and pieces of Nate's history.

Whether it was the look on Matty's face—something between a smile and a smirk—or whether my sudden bitterness rose from the fact that he was leaving me, from the sight of all his belongings boxed up and ready to move, something started sparking in my guts, a crackle of resentment for this game we'd been playing for years. I'd brought the lighter down as a gift, by damn, not a payment.

"This," I said, slipping it into my pocket, "this is mine."

Matty nodded and I knew that this too would have a price. If he remembered some pact between kids, he'd want to keep Nate's secret, hold on to a sacred bond with the brother he'd lost. That way, he'd have a memory of Nate that was his alone, and as much as I wanted that for Matty, or as much as I should have wanted it, the thought tripped a mine of jealousy in me. Dammit, I thought, I shouldn't have to pay for it. Shouldn't have to pay a red cent. He's *mine*. Nate's my son. "Where'd he hide them," I said, "the braces."

Matty turned back to his boxes. He was leaving me. He already had. "I don't remember," he said. "Somewhere."

The year Matty left his crutches at home, two weeks before Christmas, Anne and I had it out over the dogs and the dirt bike. She was peeling potatoes at the kitchen table, her hands working furiously, independently of her eyes, which were locked on mine, keeping me from the evening paper.

"Matty can't take care of a dog," I said. "Much less two. He's too young."

"But Nate's old enough for a motorbike? Christ, Tom. At least the dogs are free. Mrs. Burke says they're house-trained and gentle and good with kids. And Matty *needs* them. They'll get him out of the house more often. He's the palest seven-year-old I've ever seen."

"Get Matty the dogs," Nate said, walking in from the back hallway. He stood with a hand on the refrigerator door. "I'll help take care of them."

Anne gave him a little wink. "See there," she said, "Nate will help out," as if that settled it.

Here's a confession you don't hear too often: even parents have favorites, one child that pulls at our heart or bolsters our pride or simply reminds us the least of the things we despise in ourselves. For Anne, that child was Nate, and though she loved Matty, loved him as any mother loves a son, crippled or otherwise, it was Nate who found her eyes the heaviest and most often upon him. Perhaps because each time she saw Matty limp or pull off his prosthetic foot, it cracked her heart a little wider. Or maybe it had nothing to do with Matty. Perhaps her love for Nate was simply four years older, but I don't believe it. I never have. By the time Matty was five or six, if he had his socks and shoes off, he couldn't have limped around the room fast enough to catch up with Anne's averted eyes. Anne would protect him fiercely, from other kids, from the unkind word, even from Nate, but when it came time for the choice, I have to believe Nate would have won out. He had grown up right, and strong, and whole, the way Anne had known he would.

That night, after our argument in the kitchen, she joined me under the quilts, put her head on my chest and let out a moan I'd come to know. "Oh, yeah?" I said. "Somebody need a little roughhousing?"

Beneath the sheets, she cupped me and gave me a playful squeeze. "Now," she said, "you going to agree to the dogs or do I have to use force?"

Her hands were cold, and her hold on me sent an electric chill arcing through me from tailbone to temples. "We do the dogs," I said, "we've got to get the dirt bike, too. Nate heard everything we said, you can bet on that. The dogs, the bike, the whole shebang. That kid's sly, probably stuck up for Matty just to increase his own odds."

Anne loosened her grip a bit and turned her head, propping her chin up on my ribs while she thought it over. "Touché," she said, rolling onto me. "You've got a deal, mister."

Tonight at the wake, Lonnie's mother shook my hand, then stared me dead while I offered my condolences. She didn't say a word, and I was surprised and almost disappointed by her restraint, by her ability to keep the blame in check, to stay cool and quiet with all that grief sizzling away inside. The casket was polished and shining and closed, and while I stood against the back wall, wondering how soon I could leave without showing any disrespect, Big Red leaned next to me and exhaled hard, the gin heavy on his breath. He was wearing a suit, his tie in one of those enormous Windsor knots, but his trademark red beard was scraggly as always.

"Oh, man," he said. "You meet the mother yet?"

I nodded, and he shook his head, his eyes rolling drunk and loose in their sockets. "What gets me, Tom, is there's nothing in that box. Nothing left of him, you know? There can't be."

Later, I followed Red outside and stood under the front awning while he smoked a cigarette. He'd run out of matches, so I handed him the lighter I'd been carrying with me since I'd retrieved it from the attic. I'd polished it, replaced the flint and wick, and filled it with fuel.

Red flipped it open, lit his cigarette, and blew smoke from his nose. "Do me a favor?" he said.

"What's that?"

"Come up to the mill with me. I'm a little sauced to be running the debarker alone."

On Christmas morning, when we led the boys out to the barn, Anne teased them with the latch, saying it was stuck, letting them squirm awhile with excitement before swinging the doors open. Inside, the two dogs were curled up under Nate's new blue Honda CR80. They were full grown — half Lab, half golden — one with copper fur that seemed to shine even in the dim dawn light of the barn, the other a dull yellow thing with huge drooping eyes. Both were female, but Matty insisted on naming them Bo and Luke after his favorite TV characters.

"That's stupid," Nate told him, rolling his eyes. "Those are guy names."

"I know," Matty said, using Luke's long red tail like a whip to swat his brother. "But they like it. They're tomboys."

Within a month, Matty and the dogs were inseparable. They walked him to the bus stop in the morning, announced his return with a melody of mismatched howls in the afternoon, and slept huddled together at the foot of his bed each night. And as Nate became a better rider and began letting Matty ride behind him on the Honda, the dogs would trail them, running and barking all the way up to the forest's edge at the Petit Jean River. Weekends, I'd pay the boys with gas money for washing my truck. Inspecting their work, I'd squat down beside the rear fender wells and point out the missed spots that I pretended to see. "I don't know, boys," I'd say. "You may have to do this quarter panel all over again."

"Come on, Dad," they'd say. "You *promised*."

I never let them off easy. I wanted to have those minutes with them before they rode off to the woods. Today, if I could have them back, I'd keep them there in that driveway, scrubbing that truck indefinitely. And though in time they would recognize the injustice, and call me on it, and surely come to hate me for it, still I would persist, but in those days, when to my mind lost time could be counted in hours or days, I had little to lose by letting them go. "All right," I'd say, handing them each a dollar. "Just be careful."

Late that winter the clouds stretched solid and low from horizon to horizon and the pine branches hanging over the highway sagged under the weight of their ice-laden bark.

At the mill, the workers huddled around propane heaters, and the planers had to be honed daily to prevent them from biting jagged chunks out of the frozen logs the men pushed through the blades.

Just before the five o'clock shift change, Anne called. Her voice was quaking, panicked in a way that sent my blood to drumming in my ears. "The boys," she said. "They took the bike out, Tom. I told them not to, but I was working in the kitchen and I didn't hear them. Jesus, Tom, they've been gone for hours."

"What do you mean, hours?"

"*Hours*, Tom. God, I didn't want to bother you."

"Call the sheriff," I said. "The ranger station."

"I thought they'd come right back."

"Anne, just *call*."

I remember concentrating on the road. Sheets of ice kept blowing from the trees and slapping against the windshield. In the dark of winter dusk, the night seemed to narrow in on me, and as I roared down the hills into the valley ahead it swallowed the light of my headlamps.

The police found them the next morning near the bank of the Petit Jean, and later, at the station, a bearded deputy with deep-set eyes slid the pictures from the accident report one by one across an unfinished pine desk. The Honda was on its side, bent and buried in the brush near where a washed-out trail met the water. Nate hadn't flown far. He was twisted under the towering oak that had stopped him cold, his head snapped forward under his chest, his arms barely distinguishable from the tangle of roots at the base of the trunk.

There were no pictures of Matty. They had found him first, followed the high-pitched whining of the dogs right to him. He'd flown farther than Nate, to the water's edge at a bend in the river. He'd shattered a kneecap and cracked two ribs in the fall, but it was the cold that would have killed him.

"Dipped into the digits last night," said the officer who met us at the hospital. "And him laid out like that on the frozen riverbank, it's a wonder, it surely is, but when we pulled those dogs off him he wasn't even shivering."

The town paper made the dogs out as heroes, but Anne couldn't look at them, wouldn't let them in the house anymore. The night after the funeral, I found her sitting alone in the barn. "How could they?" she said. "How could they save Matty and leave Nate for dead?"

"Honey, they just know. It's animal instinct. They can smell the difference."

"You don't know he was dead."

"Anne, the doctors said."

"You don't *know*, Tom," she said, her bloodshot eyes swimming deep in their sockets, looking for something to blame, and rather than sympathy, what I felt that night was rage. She didn't know either, couldn't know, and that's what was gnawing at her. She hadn't seen it coming, hadn't been able to hear it in the wind the way she could hear the next

day's rain, but what frightened me most was my convic-
tion that, in Anne's mind, the wrong boy had been taken
from her. Something welled up in me, molten and slow.
The dogs were whining, scratching at the back door, and
our surviving son was alone in his bed upstairs.

"Dogs know, Anne. I don't, you're right, but dogs do.
What did you want, huh? For them to let the crippled one
die?"

Since she left, I've spent hours on the porch, subjecting
myself to the cold, mulling that night over and wondering
how I could have said what I did. And when I'm brave with
whiskey and honest with myself, I begin to suspect the ug-
liest possible answer, that I deserved the stab of her stare
and have earned, in that one fit of rage, these biting nights
I've endured, even nights like tonight, when the blame in
Lonnie's mother's eyes was as sharp and cold as Anne's had
been. That it was me, not Anne, who wanted Nate back so
badly. No matter the cost.

We kept Matty home from school for a week after the accident. At night, the dogs howled at the door, and Anne
grew more and more remote, sinking so far into herself
that I prayed she'd slam a door or throw something or beat
me with her fists, anything so I could recognize her as the
woman I'd taken as my wife.

Afternoons, I'd load Matty up in the truck and haul him
up to the top of Magazine Mountain. A fire had crowned
up there in the sixties, the regrowth was sparse and low to
the ground, and we'd walk around up there, staring out at

the waves of clouds that rolled out in all directions below us. His ribs were taped, his good leg now stiff and clumsy in its cast, but he never much complained. He'd hobble around in his old arm braces, which he preferred to the wooden crutches they'd given him at the hospital, and when he moved there was an unhurried calm about him. Weeks later, when the cast came off, he walked with his head up and his shoulders squared, confident and almost proud of the hitch in his step, and I realized then that, in a way, Matty had embraced his limp as a reminder, as a way of mourning.

Back home, more and more, Anne was coming undone. The dogs, now deprived of their warm and huddled sleep at the foot of Matty's bed, spent the nights scratching and sniffing at the back door, whining to be let in. It drove her crazy, Anne said. She couldn't sleep.

One morning, while Matty and I were eating breakfast before our ride to the mountain, she emerged from the bedroom. If you'd been there, you might have wondered just what had become of this woman. Her shoulders slumped forward, some invisible burden pressing hard on her, and her eyes were cast down and away, as if inspecting the baseboards for dust. "Mommy," Matty said, but Anne held up a hand. She'd woken me four times the night before, muttering and climbing from bed and pacing in and out of the bedroom, slapping her hands over her ears when the dogs launched a new vocal assault on the door. Now she poured a cup of coffee and stood facing the sink, and when, from out on the porch, the dogs bellowed, her body jolted, something electric pulsing through her, and her hands shook violently enough that coffee splashed over the rim of the cup and onto her hands.

"*Shut up,*" she screamed, stomping her way toward the utility room and the back door. "Enough. That's enough out there. Just shut up."

From my chair at the table, I heard the deadbolt snap back and the door swing open. "Anne," I said.

Matty's eyes were on me, his fork frozen above his plate, and the dogs were howling.

"*No,*" Anne said, "*stay.*" And then the door slammed shut, or nearly shut, and the house shook and there was that same hollow sound I'd heard all those years back at Uncle Weldon's slaughterhouse in Texas, that sledgehammer coming down, making contact, that calf dropping limp into the dust, and I kicked my chair back just as Anne started ranting.

"You're not allowed," she said. "You're not allowed inside. Oh, Jesus, you know that."

When I made it around to the door, Anne was standing there, her hands knotted up in her nightgown, her hair limp and dirty as the dog lying at her feet. It was Luke, her shiny red coat now dulled and tangled from all the days out of doors. She was still wedged between the heavy oak door and the doorjamb, her head dented in at the temples. "She was trying to get in," Anne said. "I didn't mean it. I didn't mean it, but she wouldn't stop."

Matty rounded the corner, fork still in hand, and when

he looked down at his dog and then up at me, he seemed older somehow, already a man, shrunken and beaten down by years of misfortune. "Daddy," he said, and I took his hand and pulled him past Anne and onto the back porch. "She's still breathing," I told him, pulling the dog from the doorway. "Let's get her in the truck. We'll take her over to Dr. Mason's."

Anne stood crying on the porch, watching us load the dog into the cab. Whether determined to accompany her sister or terrified by the prospect of staying behind, or both, the other dog, Bo, leapt into the bed of the truck, and when we climbed in and slammed the doors, Luke opened her eyes. "She's okay," Matty said, and I nodded, forcing a smile, but the dog's eyes were deep pools of black, dilated so that only the faintest rim of white was left visible. Before we made it out to the highway, the dog jerked, her muscles seizing up so that her legs shot forward, her nails scratching across the dash of the truck, and what I remember most is not the sound of the dog's jaw snapping shut, or the way the last rush of breath pushed from the poor thing's flared nostrils, or the way Bo was whining in the back, her nose pressed hard into the glass of the cab. Not even the way Matty leaned forward, covering the dog's body with his own. No, what I remember most is the sight of Anne out there on the porch before we drove away, the way she just stood there, her legs and arms pale from all her time indoors, her lips moving in whispered thoughts I'd never be able to hear. She was my wife, and I'd cursed her as I put the truck in gear, and then she'd turned back toward the house. She wiped her feet on the mat before she went in, and I knew she was leaving.

When we got to the mill, Red and I ran the hoses and cranked up the power washer, and out there in the night, with the clouds and the cold and the silence working a number on us, we stood at the infeed side of the debarker drum, spraying the insides clean with a hot mix of ammonia and water. The smell, Red had told me at the funeral home, had gotten worse each day, so he'd called an old buddy of his, Henderson, the line foreman at our sister plant in Silsbee, Texas, for advice.

"They had possums," Red said, "a whole family of them nesting nights. Henderson said they fired up one morning and debarked at least a half dozen of the little bastards. Said the only thing that made a dent in the stench was a good hose-down and a couple drum-loads of cedar."

So we worked. We sprayed and vapor rose from the water to join the clouds and soon enough the drum was steaming like a kiln, but the smell was still there, rank and sour, swirling out of that drum into the air. I couldn't shake it, it hung in my nostrils, but not once did I think, *That's a man. That's a man I'm smelling.*

At the time, all I could think about was Matty's dog, Luke, who I'd buried that day, in anger and disbelief, beneath the plot of ground where Anne had always made her garden. I'd bent my back and shoveled for an hour, digging down deep while Matty sat on the porch, holding Bo's head in his hands to keep her quiet, and by the time I'd finished Anne had packed the car with her clothes and some groceries for the trip. She was going back to Texas, she said. To her mother's. I slid the dog into the hole, and the solid sound it made hitting bottom kicked the air from my lungs. I turned to Matty on the porch, a boy holding fast to his dog, a boy too frightened to cry, and when my breath came back to me I boiled over. I told Anne to go on, then, if that's what she wanted, if she wanted to leave her family behind, if she thought she could just hop in the car and drive away from her life. "Just go the hell on," I said, and then I packed the earth back over that dog.

Now Red was feeling better. Sobering up some, he said. He could drive. And though I shouldn't have allowed it, I knew that, for Red, this job would never be done if he couldn't see it through. He'd flipped the switch, and as crazy and insensitive and downright impossible as it sounds, Red was a company man, and by the unspoken rules of the mill, this was his wrong to right. So while he was on the cherry picker, rolling out past the fence to the raw materials yard for the cedar, I fired up the infeed conveyor. The belt was riding high on one side of its idlers, so I worked a wrench on the take-ups to train it back straight, and when Red drove up with the first of the logs, I stepped down to the debarker's control panel and fired the thing up. Once released, the logs crashed down, bouncing on the impact idlers before the belt shot them forward into the drum, and then I engaged the drive shaft. Red was just sitting there on the cherry picker smoking a cigarette, and I was eleven years back and five miles away, in my backyard with Matty, who was balanced on one of his braces, pointing to where his dog was digging. It was Bo, hunkered in a hole of her own making, tunneling down to where two weeks before I'd buried Luke. "She remembers," Matty said, and his braces rattled while he sobbed. "She wants Luke back."

And what do you say to that? *Yes, she does, son. She surely does.* Something as simple and stupid and inadequate as that, and then you just stand there, holding on to your boy while he cries, watching while the dog slings soil, digging deeper. You're not thinking about decay, about the smell of rot. You're thinking about the son you have left and the son who died because of a dirt bike you bought him and the wife who told you so, who told you so when she turned to go. That dog, the one underground, it's the last thing on your mind, until it hits you, a stench so bad your boy rears back on his braces, a smell so dead you grab the digging dog and wrench her by the collar out of that hole, because this isn't right, not with the boy here, it isn't, because he's had enough lessons like this for a lifetime, you think, and that's when you send him inside. That's when you head for the barn, grab the bags of Ready-Crete you keep for setting new fence posts, and dam that hole up for good. And then it's done.

"That ought to do it," Red shouted. "I think that'll do it, Tom."

I shut the debarker down and the logs rolled loud like summer thunder to a stop inside. Red stepped down from the cherry picker and stood beside me at the controls. And then I kicked on the pneumatics and opened the discharge vents. I'm forty-seven years old, I've been in lumber mills half my life, but when those vents sprang clear and that bark dust flew, I nearly went teary with relief. It came in gusts, wafting toward us, wave after wave of cedar so sharp and clean and loud that it left your sinuses ringing.

"Jesus God," Red said. "Oh *Lord*, that's better."

I killed the pneumatics and we stood there together, taking it in, our breath steaming. "I think that did it," Red said. "I think it's all right now." He was breathing hard, his cheeks flushed with the gin or the cold or both.

You were drunk at a man's wake, I thought. *Whatever guilt you've got worming around in you, this won't get rid of it.*

He looked at me, his a tired smile. The man was still wearing his tie. He pulled my lighter from his pocket, lit a cigarette, and handed the thing back to me. I turned it in my hand, gave the flint wheel a turn, and the flame came to life. I flipped it shut and looked up to find Red smiling, his face lit up with relief, and I knew then that I'd go home and have one last drink on the porch, that I'd sit and sip my whiskey out there, and then I'd take my sad, shivering ass back into the house and call my son. I'd call my son and when he answered I'd tell him I was mailing him a package, the old lighter I'd refused him before—that and some pocket change—and when he asked me what I wanted, I'd tell him. *Nothing*, I'd say. *Nothing, son. I don't want anything at all.* There would be something like silence, a static hiss, our breath crackling inside hundreds of miles of frozen telephone lines. He wouldn't say thank you. I didn't expect he'd say anything at all, but then I'd change my mind. *There is something,* I'd say. *How you doing out there anyway. How's school, I mean. Tell me about you, son. I want to hear about you.*

"Yes, sir," Red said, still breathing deep through his nose, "that's a whole shitpot better."

In every way a man can know something — from experience, from his gut, from the sound of the wind, from the smell of pine trees and from the voice he sometimes hears in his head when he prays — in all those ways I knew Red was wrong, that it would take more than one night of work out in the cold to bring him relief. And still I wanted to believe. I wanted it to be true, for it to be over. For both of us.

"Let's do this right," I said, nodding toward the cherry picker, then out beyond the fence to where the cedar was stacked. "One more load, just to be sure. Then I've got to get home."

Because He Can't Not Remember

FIVE MINUTES MORE and the Ramirez twins will be rifling through her purse while they weave through traffic on Highway 225, Raul's foot heavy on the gas as they put time and miles between themselves and the gringa they've left bloodied and unconscious, laid out on her back in the Walmart parking lot.

Five minutes more and this is the way Tim Tilden will lose his wife, but now, as he steers his Chevy S-10 off the 225 feeder road and into the Walmart parking lot, the only thing he fears losing is his ever-loving mind. Diapers, by damn. Midnight and they need diapers. Beside him in his car seat, little Timmy is sleeping through all his mother's banter—and man, oh man, can this woman cause grief with her mouth. Put her on a northbound bus, she'd talk the ears off a couple counties of Iowa cornfields, guaran-

teed. Tonight, Tim's thinking, she's nothing but piss vinai-
grette and a will that every thought to cross her mind be
heard at higher decibels. Insisted, for chrissake, that she
come along, haul the baby out after midnight. And why?
More time to talk. Yak the entire way, bellyaching about
sore nipples and soaked bras. Tit-talk, Tim calls it — and
not the kind a man can appreciate, either.

About all they can figure, Tim and Natalie, is that the
kid can't stand the taste of skin, the sting of salt. Gets
spooked like a puppy at a pistol range, maybe by the faintest sounds of human plumbing, blood on the move beneath
flesh — who knows? — but he's two weeks old today and
still he won't nurse. Turns his head from Natalie's breast
like maybe it's bared teeth at him and gone to growling.
Back home in Deer Park, some three miles away in a rent-
house neighborhood near the ship channel, the top shelf of
their refrigerator is stacked two rows deep with boiled Ball
jars full of extra pumped breast milk. The sound these last
few nights — the electric pump whirring, applying relief to
his wife — reminds Tim of the throttly purr of their tabby,
a sneaky beast that, given the chance, would find a fast
home for every ounce of that stuff. The cat, Tim thinks.
The cat would fucking nurse.

And now, after two weeks' worth of worry, here he is,
cooped up in his truck with his wife, and she's got her
mouth kicked into overdrive. It's like that with Natalie,
hop in the cab and prepare for the gab. Two years back,
when they'd only just caught fire as a couple, after that
first weekend of shit-kicking at the Gypsum Road Saloon,

after the long, sheet-tangling nights at Tim's apartment, Tim had taken a liking to her constant chitchat, to the leathery feel of the steering wheel and the smell of that jasmine perfume she kept heavy on her neck. She'd roll down the window and pull her skirt up on her thighs, and then she'd let it roll, miles of the most meaningless stuff a man could ever hope to hear: the gossip from the car dealership where she still did the filing and answered phones—who was getting slippery with who down in the service department's grease pit, getting serviced something fierce, she'd say, amidst used oil filters and the slick smell of 10W-40. Shit like that. Hell, get a few longnecks in her and she'd even talk to the traffic, to the stoplights. "Turn me loose," she once screamed, hanging out the window and giving the long red light on Canal an exaggerated, nail-polished finger. They were on the way home from the Gypsum, where Natalie had pronounced the end of their dance night by cupping him under the table and downing the rest of his beer. "You don't give me the green here, I'm gonna come unglued with horny."

Yeah, sure, Tim had liked it, had liked the way she rode close to him, straddling the gear shift, her hips next to his on the bench seat, had liked the throaty moan she'd made when he shifted down into fourth on the entrance ramp. Lately, though, between the kid raising Cain and the calls from Natalie's mother telling them to hold out, that the kid would nurse when he got good and hungry and angry enough to suck hard—between all that mess and Natalie's mile-a-minute mouth, he's had about e-goddamn-nough.

At least, he thinks, riding the clutch before the turn, right now she's talking some truth, some honest motherly words, words about fear, and though he's grown tired of her chatter, at least for now she's making sense.

"I swear he's scared of it," Natalie says. "Such a big old thing stuck right in his little face."

Turning into the crowded parking lot, Tim cracks the window to let her words out. Another Houston night so hot and humid you could hang teabags from tree branches to steep. A night gone ripe with the sulfur-sweet stink of the Exxon and Shell and Phillips plants lining the highway. From here at the Walmart, it all looks too organized. The way the little warning lights flash in sync atop the condensate tanks, the way the smokestacks fill the sky with what looks like a regulated stream of gray-green smoke.

"He ain't scared," Tim says, steering toward the center lane of parking spaces. "Not a man on the planet would be scared of pontoons like yours, never mind his age."

"Well, he sure enough *acts* scared. And he ain't scared of the bottle, Tim. He's not one bit scared of that."

Tim knows it's true: put the stuff in a bottle and the little guy will latch on like a Louisiana leech, but that's not what troubles him most.

No, what really worries him is this homo gene he's read about.

At work, delivering mail on his route, Tim has all the free reading he likes. On his morning trip to the post office can, on his coffee breaks at ten and two, even on his lunch break, he's taken to reading the newspapers and magazines he's yet to deliver. For the first year or so, he'd take his pocketknife to the plastic wrap of someone's *Playboy* or *Penthouse*, spend his break time comparing Natalie to the airbrushed angels of the world, but lately he's gotten down to educating himself in things other than glossy pink skin. That's how he sees it, this reading—an education. The only one he'll ever get this side of his degree from Channelview High. Lately, though, it's this education that's got him to fretting, and he's sick with the thought that maybe his kid's not right in the wrist, that maybe there's a scientific reason the little guy won't nurse. He's read it somewhere, how when you're a queer, you're born that way, and though it all seems as impossibly strange as the crowd of midnight traffic in this parking lot, he can't put a stop to the thoughts. Little Timmy in leather pants with both ears pierced, introducing Mom and Dad to his new *friend*. Sick shit, Tim thinks.

Searching for a spot, Tim steers wide to the left around the rear of an old beat-to-hell Buick that's jutting out from its parking space. A car with a heavy, twisted bumper, pulled out jagged-like on one side by a previous collision. He eases down on the brake and waits while, six or seven spaces from the front of the store, taillights come to life on a Dodge van. When it backs out, he makes a sharp right into the spot. Beside him, Natalie's breathing hard through her nose, her face furrowed with worry. She pulls the sleeping baby from the car seat, holds him under his bottom and cradles him close before handing him to Tim and snatching her purse from beneath the seat.

"I don't know how he can sleep," she says. "He's soaked clean through. How'd we ever run out of diapers, anyway?"

Tim rocks the little guy in his arms awhile, amazed as always by the kid's weight. Almost nothing. Seems lighter than the JCPenney Christmas catalogues he delivers each October. When he climbs from the cab, he waits for Natalie to make her way around the bed of the truck.

"I just don't get it," she says, straightening her purse strap on her shoulder.

"We just ran out," Tim says, his voice too full of impatience. "It's bound to be my fault. That much I'm sure of."

Natalie shoots him one of her more matrimonial looks. "Not that," she says. "I mean, one time when I was barely in high school, I flew up to Tulsa to see Grandma Lawson and there was this woman sitting behind me on the plane with her baby. Well, at the time I'm not exactly looking forward to some squalling brat sitting behind me, but when we take off the kid's just as quiet as he could be, you know?"

Tim shuts the door gentle-like, gives it a final nudge with his hip. "Like this?" he says, nodding down at the baby.

"Yeah," she says, sliding her hand into the back pocket of his Wranglers as they head toward the store. "I mean, I know he's a good kid, sleeps like a champ, but that's not what I'm talking about. What I'm talking about is that, after a couple minutes, I'm sitting there on the plane reading my magazine and I feel this shot of something warm in my hair. I just barely feel it, you know, like when someone's standing right behind you in line at the Safeway and you can feel their breath in your hair? But then it happens again, and when I turn around this woman isn't even embarrassed. She's just sitting there smiling with this little tit poking out of her blouse. She's kinda shaking her head and looking at me while this baby is sucking at her like some kind of newborn Hoover, and I mean going *berzerk*, Tim. *Really* sucking. So hard he can't keep up with the stream. So hard that all of a sudden, when it's too much for him, when he's gotta catch his breath, he jerks his head back and the milk goes flying, and the woman, she's just laughing, looking over at her husband who's beaming down like he's Joseph and the three kings have just forked over the frankincense and myrrh, and there I am with some strange woman's milk in my hair. And do you know what she finally says to me?"

"I hope to God she *uddered* an apology," Tim says. He leans hard on the word, but Natalie doesn't bite, doesn't seem to notice at all.

"Not even close. She just kinda shrugs it off and says, 'He gets so greedy when he's hungry.' That's what I'm talking about, Tim. That's what I want."

Pulling into the parking lot, without looking down, the Ramirez twins stab their cigarettes out in the overflowing ashtray. Raul steers slowly up the side drive toward the front doors, scanning the parking lot.

Fucking midnight, he thinks, and look at this. Too busy. Too many cars. People.

"Just relax," Jesus says. "Just drive."

It's always been like this. Jesus was born first, ten minutes, and their mother says he came out breech, his arms thrown over his head like he was reaching up for Raul. Ever since, it's as if he's decided never to let go again. When it comes to his twin, Jesus refuses to miss out on anything, even a thought. He hears them all.

Strange as it is, Raul doesn't mention Jesus' hold on him, not to his younger brother, Eduardo. Not to the gringos he sweats with six days a week, hunched beneath the sun tying iron, lacing and weaving rebar up on that half-finished bridge so the mixers can pour the concrete. His day job. The one that pays rent, buys groceries. The rest—the stereo and the new blue paint for the LeMans, the two-tone roach-killer shoes like the old Pachucos used to wear—it's all from these rides with Jesus. Jesus who knows everything. Everything. What he's thinking, man.

About this, he tells only Monica. Because she licks her lips when she listens. Because she shines, brown like new pennies. Because she keeps her fingernails long and red and runs them together like a rake through his pubic hair when he's finished. For her, he'll tell, and one night he does. He gives her ear a little bite, leans in close to whisper it. "He hears what's between my ears, baby. Motherfucker always knows. Always."

"When you think about me?" she says. "Even then?"

He runs his tongue down the outer ridge of her ear. "And when would that be, baby?"

Now Jesus points, says, "Quit thinking 'bout your little split-tail, man. Business before putas, vato. Look here, what we got."

And there they are, easy pickings, coming up on Raul's side of the car. It's luck of the draw, he knows, but twice this month they've been on his side, no time to circle around, so he has to snatch *and* drive.

He takes his foot off the gas, lets the Pontiac ride the idle. "You crazy? They got a baby, man."

"*She* don't. All she gots is a purse."

Years later, Tim Tilden will teach his boy to drive. He'll rush home from a hot day spent cooped up in his mail Jeep and watch his son's fluid fadeaway move beneath the basketball hoop he'd mounted on the garage for the kid's twelfth birthday, when Timmy insisted he be called Tim, just Tim, like his father who now, fifteen years after Natalie's death, will stand there in the driveway jingling his truck keys in his hand, wondering how many times she would have confused them both by calling their shared name, how many times they both would have answered from the living room when she piped up from the kitchen, "Tim, could you give me a hand in here?"

After the boy shoots his final jump shot, rimming it in, he'll turn to his father, wink, and grab his shirt from beside the old metal garbage cans where he'd thrown it an hour before. Tim will look at his son, at the man he's become, at the hard muscles of his shoulders and the confidence of his long strides. He'll smile at the idea that, way back when, he'd questioned a newborn's masculinity.

Father and son, they'll carry the cans out to the street, pace off ten steps and set the cans next to the curb, thirty feet apart. In the truck, Tim Tilden will show the boy the basics of parallel parking. He'll explain that this is where the SOBs get you, that this is the part of the driving test where most people lose their cool, that it's all confidence and finesse, and that any man worth his weight can do it with his eyes closed. The boy will line the truck up, stretch his arm across the seat top as he looks back, angling between the cans, and when he begins to straighten up, he'll wink once more at his father. He'll be in, first try, no problem, but when he moves his foot for the brake, something will go wrong. He'll miss. He'll catch the corner of the accelerator with his foot, and the lightest tap on the gas will push the truck back into the can. When it crashes onto its side, the boy will sit there in disbelief, amazed by the noise the damn thing makes, puzzled at the sight of his father, who will have closed his eyes against the sharp sound of impact, and who will keep them closed while the trash can lid rolls across the street, throwing sunlight from its surface while it whirls, in a clanging, oblong spin, to a stop.

"Grab hold with both hands," Jesus says, "and punch it. I'll take the wheel." Raul nods, but his head, Jesus knows, isn't in the game. It's the same every time. He's worried about witnesses, imagining handcuffs and some HPD jail cell, eyeing a group of teenagers who are flirting and smoking just outside the Walmart doors. He's thinking, They've got us pegged. They're watching.

"Don't worry about them," Jesus says. "Just kids, vato."

Still, Raul isn't moving, so Jesus gives him a knuckle thump hard on the side of his head. "I said don't *worry* about it. I got us covered."

An hour before, Jesus had swapped the plates on Raul's LeMans with a pair he'd stolen a year ago from a late-model Nissan. He'd been on his way to the beach in Surfside when he noticed the car abandoned on the side of Highway 288, not far from the lockdown in Rosharon. It had been a solitary thrill, one full of senseless risk, a slap in the face of those HPD shit kickers who so often put him and his boys against cars or walls and kicked their feet apart and frisked them in their east-side streets. In a way, it felt like the first time he'd snatched the belt from his mother's hand when he was twelve, and told Raul to get outside, and looked the old woman square in the face and told her she wouldn't do that—not to Raul, she wouldn't—not anymore, because it could suck the life out of the boy and because there was something sick about it, swinging leather at your own flesh and blood, and because, from now on, if Raul got out of line, Jesus and no one but Jesus would handle it.

Yes, it seemed the same somehow, to pull up behind that car, to step down from his truck with his tool kit and feel the swirl in his stomach from his three-beer breakfast, to turn the screws and yank the plates while tanker trucks blew by on their way to the coast and while, less than half a mile away, prisoners worked the fields as armed guards on horseback spit tobacco into the broken soil.

They are safe, no plates to trace, but still, Raul doesn't look convinced. He wears worry up high on the ridge of his eyebrows, and Jesus thinks maybe he'll blow their chance, but at the last minute Raul turns the wheel to the left, veering toward the couple as they approach the store. Raul looks his brother hard in the eye, then turns and slings his arm casually out the window as they rumble nearer, and Jesus hears his brother mapping it out in his head. *Easy now. Come up on them slowly. Just like before. Reel her in. Grab the purse and go.*

What the hell is *this*, Tim thinks. The car, it's coming up on them, shining and blue and so close that in a second or two the driver, a Mexican with his eyes locked on Natalie, will be able to reach out and touch her if he wants, maybe cop a feel before speeding away. Perverts, Tim thinks. Perverts at the goddamn Walmart.

But something's not right. Tim knows it by the way Natalie's fingers clench in the back pocket of his Wranglers, by the way the guy in the passenger seat leans into view with a tight smile on his face, by the sudden, cool slicks of sweat in his armpits. Then the outstretched arm, the driver reaching for her, and there's not a thing in the world Tim can do. He's holding the baby. He's holding the baby and he can't let go and the engine revs so loud that when Natalie's hand wrenches back in his pocket Tim thinks at first it's the noise itself, the goddamn sound of the thing, that's spinning him around.

And then—*Jesus Christ*, she's sliding. She's sliding alongside the car.

Before Raul sees the fear on her face, before he braces himself and puts his foot down hard on the gas, what he notes is the purse strap in his hands, the thin band of leather that links him to this woman who only now, when he kicks the accelerator and tightens his grasp, seems to recognize what's happening, her eyes frozen somewhere between surprise and panic. Raul feels the air, hot and solid and rushing in the windows, pushing him back in his seat. He keeps on the gas while Jesus leans in close, taking the wheel, and Raul knows that something's gone wrong. Too much weight on the other end, too much pull, and outside the window, where there should be nothing but asphalt and parked cars and a purse flapping wild in the night, she's there instead—the woman, one shoulder jammed tight against the door of his car, just inches from his hands, hung up in the strap of her purse, her eyes fixed hard on him. He hears it, the sound of her, the hiss of fabric and skin giving way to asphalt.

She's struggling to get free, but what Raul sees is a woman fighting him, the *pinche gringa*, and he tightens his hold as the car gains speed and the leather bites into the palms of his hands and he thinks for sure he's bleeding. He looks up and Jesus nods, smiling, yes, but only from the corners of his mouth, and then Raul sees the car parked

crooked in its space ahead, the way it's jutting out into his
path, its bumper crumpled and sharp and coming up fast.
And the woman is still there, eyeballing him, begging him
with a blank-eyed stare to stop. It's you, he thinks. It's you,
puta. Let. Fucking. Go.

"No," Jesus says, because he hears everything. What's
between his ears, vato, but this time he's misunderstood.
"Hold on, Raul," he says, and Raul hangs on.

They all do.

They have taken his wife. They have taken her and he's
standing here motionless watching them, holding on to his
son. Not doing a goddamn thing. He's seen the scowls of
their faces and the hint of a smile from the one who reached
over to grab the wheel. He's felt her hand clench tight in
his back pocket when they took her, heard the denim rip
at the seam when it gave and she went sliding away. And
now—oh Lord, now as her head is cracked wide by the
bumper of that junkyard car, Tim can only imagine what
might have been. Not the future and the years they might
have had together—impossible now, he knows—but the
way he had seen them and the things he should have done.
He imagines himself stepping between Natalie and the car,
lunging down hard on the driver's arm just as he reaches
out for her purse. He imagines hearing the sound of it, not
his wife's head hammering hard against steel, but the echo
of the driver's arm snapping at the elbow under his weight.

Raul feels the shock of her impact in the socket of his
shoulder, a single jolt of resistance that pulls him out the

window up to his waist, and then they're free. He's held on. He's got the purse, and when he pulls himself back into the driver's seat and squeals the tires onto the feeder road, Raul's pulse is louder in his ears than the engine. His fingers are tingling and he can't feel the steering wheel and there's this emptiness opening wide inside, hollowing him out, a kind of hunger he knows he'll never keep fed. "They gonna bring us down, Jesus. Holy shit, man, this is it. They gonna find us. They ain't ever gonna stop looking."

Jesus lights a cigarette, tilts the rearview so he can look his brother in the eyes. He takes hold of Raul's leg, squeezing him hard above the knee. "They ain't gonna find shit," he says. "Ain't gonna be nothing to find. Swap the plates, ditch the purse, keep our mouths shut. What they gonna find?"

Then they're on the highway, swerving through traffic on their way back toward I-10 east and their neighborhood just inside the loop, where there are still bodegas instead of Stop-N-Gos, where the smell of fried masa means you're only blocks or feet from where you sleep. Raul imagines that he's already in bed, the smells swirling in through the open windows, and he's holding on to Monica, trying to tell her lies about the night and what he's done. But his blood—oh, man, it's still thrumming something ugly inside, and he can't do it, so he sits up in bed and comes clean with it, tells her about the six dollars they got from the gringa's purse, shares a cigarette he bought with her Texaco card, whispers what it looked like in the rearview mirror. The woman, deflated and out cold on her back and so still, everything still but the steam coming up from the asphalt.

"You ain't gonna tell her nothing," Jesus says, still gripping his leg. "You gonna keep it all to yourself."

There is half a week's worth of her milk in the refrigerator. Three or four times each night, and a half dozen times each day, Tim Tilden will pour it from the canning jars, warm the bottle in a hot water bath on the stove, and rock the kid in the living room while he feeds him. On the last night, when there's one jar left, he'll buy formula at the corner store and drop his son at his parents' house for a few hours. He'll shake off their questions, say he's fine, just needs to be alone for a while. He'll drive to the Gypsum and down a few beers, and later, when he's sitting at the stoplight on Canal, he'll notice how quiet it is, and he'll turn the radio up—KIKK, country and western and loud. He'll sit there imagining Natalie beside him, will see her leaning out the window and flipping the bird at the light, screaming, *Turn me loose.*

He'll remember the night she died, because he can't not remember it, because it clings to him the way the smell of her jasmine perfume clings to the sheets of their bed, but what he'll recall is not the way she damn near ripped the pocket off his Wranglers, or the way it took fifteen minutes for the cops to arrive—not even the way those bastards smoked their tires getting onto the feeder road. No, what Tim will see that night, sitting alone in his truck at a long red light, is his boy latched onto his pinkie finger, sucking until it turns numb and pruned and Tim has to pluck it from his mouth, sending the kid into a fit of wailing.

Greedy, Tim will think, remembering Natalie's voice. He'll pull the last jar of her milk from beneath the seat and unscrew the cap and tilt it back. *He gets so greedy when he's hungry.*

Something for the Poker Table

Y OU'RE IMPATIENT, SOMETIMES thoughtless—a little cheap, too—so when you snag your worn and weather-checked water hose on the jagged bumper of your fifteen-year-old truck, you don't think a thing about it. You pull. You throw yourself into it, two hundred some odd pounds of man versus a single-braid hose—SBR cover, SBR tube, cheap rubber atop cheap fabric atop cheap rubber, the whole thing made by mandrels and little Korean men whose older brothers your older brother chased through jungles wet and green and alive enough to outlive them all. You curse and pull, but the sharp steel of the bent bumper digs in, won't let go. Your bum knee is giving you hell these days, you'd rather not walk the fifty paces back to the truck to free the damn thing, so you plant your good leg and lean into it. You heave and the hose squeaks and pops, tears clean in two, and when you look up again you're square on your ass between squat rows of July cotton.

Be *got-damned*, you think, if I'm buying a new hose, so you don't drive into town and call Jerry Curlee, the balding Bohemian salesman who puts forty percent into hose and baler belting and roller chain before he sells it to you. No, you go into the truck bed toolbox and fish out just what you need—a hose mender. A quick fix, by damn, so you can run this hose tonight, so you can get the creek water from the pump house to the irrigation lines, so the plants will come up green and thick despite this south Texas heat.

A hose mender, a marvel of the modern world, you think. One seven-inch length of tubing, galvanized steel or, like this one, cast brass, barbed on the ends like a tomcat's pecker. What goes in must not come out—not till the job's done, anyway. Ram one shank into each end of your ripped-in-half hose, screw some Dixon worm-gear clamps down tight on each side so it holds, and off you go. Couple it to the pump line, open the gate valve and you've got a working hose, holding pressure the way the doctors up in Houston say your anterior arteries will now that they've mended you with stents, their handiwork holding you open from the inside out, your blood slurping past that surgical steel the way now this water's starting to sluice through that brass mender.

And that deserves a cigarette. You bend yourself over one slow time, checking a plant for the tiny pearls of weevil eggs, and then you head back to lean on the truck while you light one up. You take the smoke in deep and work your tongue over your teeth while the hose holds its own and the sun leans west to kindle the horizon. When a duster buzzes in from the south, crows launch themselves from telephone lines. The plane banks hard just the other side of the farm-to-market road, dives, and you can see the pilot in there, a young guy in a baseball cap, glancing back at his wake of Malathion spray. He'll dust today for the weevils, come back in September to defoliate before the pickers move in.

It strikes you, as he cuts his spray and throttles up into his steep ascent, that we've got a reliable fix for damn near everything these days, and before you know it you're adding up all your success stories. The weekend you spent with grease to your elbows, replacing the cam bearings and hand clutch on the old Allis-Chalmers tractor you've had since you bought your first hundred acres. The barn roof you rebuilt and shingled alongside your father in a single scorching day after Hurricane Carla sucked the old one off and delivered it half a mile west to the banks of the Navidad. The calf you saved one humid night when the moon forgot to rise and Doc Vacek didn't answer his phone, the way it took you half an hour just to scare that damn heifer into the light of the barn; the way, when you saw the blood coming hard from her and the single hoof showing, you cursed yourself for cursing her. And then your boots kept sliding in the warm slop of shit and hay on the floor, sliding until you called your wife out there to help you tie the heifer off and hold her head, until you wedged yourself between the poor girl and the loft ladder and found enough purchase to work your hand and forearm up inside her. And this, this was something for the poker table, something for the feed store loading docks, something for your pal Grady Derrich to shake his head at. This was one made to be told. The real thing. You know it now and you knew it then, knew it as you worked your arm around and felt the insides of her, the slick and squeezing heat of it, knew it while you followed the soft leather of the shoulder down to the hoof and worked it out alongside the other one. Knew it as you got the calf puller rigged up, with every turn of the ratchet that set the young mother to moaning, with every quiver of her hide. And then the calf came, wide-eyed and alive, and with her more work.

You cleared the cavities, put down new hay, got the mother washed out and sewed up and the little one sucking, and then, around midnight, you could stand there smoking awhile before stripping down and hosing off just out back of the house. Afterward, on the porch in a towel, while your wife shook her head at you and handed you a cup of coffee, you told her you were sure enough glad you didn't raise elephants. You remember her laugh. You remember how it cut itself short, how she seemed always sad in the eyes those days, even that night, despite the calf you'd kept alive.

And now, now your cigarette's out and you light another one, because there's nobody around presently to tell you just how surely you're killing yourself. Thirty-nine years now you've been sucking on these things, and you guess you might as well pencil them into the *Can't Fix* side of the ledger. You lean against your truck awhile and blow smoke from your nose while the duster makes another low run, its engine drowning out the sound of the water you've set to flowing. And then it comes to you, something you haven't thought of once in your life without laughing. Until now. Somehow, even with the work all but done for the day and the sting of Malathion spray swirling familiar as cotton-seed in the air, you don't so much as smile.

Fifteen years ago, when you could still polka three songs in a row without stopping to catch your breath, in the truck—brand new that summer, and shining—with your better half, stuck in traffic on a trip to the city, your wife, she points and laughs at a billboard above. VASECTOMY RE-VERSAL, it reads. GUARANTEED. "Look, sugar," she says. "Your sperm or your money back." You smile at the thought of something so silly, a fix for something that's already been fixed, and you remember that weekend some years back, after the birth of your second son, when the doctors had sliced and tugged and tied and sent you home to sit on the couch with your nuts propped up on a towel full of ice, your newest, most daring shave itching like chiggers dropped down your underpants.

You ease ahead in traffic and shake your head. She puts a hand on your knee. She's getting older, the lines cut deeper in her knuckles, but the question she asks and the shine in her eyes let you know she's not too old. Not yet, she isn't. "So what do you think, my little gelding," she says. "Wanna untie the knot?"

It's in her eyes. It's there and you don't see it.

But now you do. Now that it's fifteen years too late. Now that your second cigarette is ashed down to the filter and there's nothing left but to drive home and let this water you've set to flowing drain itself into the earth. Now you see it just fine. Through all the long days and short nights, you see it. She's in the truck, telling you with her eyes. One more, she wants. A girl this time. Someone to dress up Sundays in frills and patent-leather shoes instead of Wranglers and ropers. And the answer you need is right there in the cab with you, no need to root through the toolbox out back in the bed, but you don't give it. No, you shake your head and write the whole thing off as a joke. You sit there in traffic with her for an hour and it never hits you. You stand all but naked on your back porch less than a year later. You're sipping coffee after pulling a calf into the world, you're making jokes and still her eyes won't light up. You're waiting—just this week at the feed store loading docks—smoking and spitting and swapping stories with Grady Derrich, your friend of forty years. You've been farming your whole life, you tell him, but you'll be damned if you can get a lasting smile to grow on that woman's face.

You're getting back into your truck, and you'll be damned, but you'd always believed she never lacked for what she needed. The crop duster makes one last pass out toward the blazing horizon, and you'll be damned.

We Don't Talk That Way in Texas

THE SUMMER I turned nine, my mother packed my suitcase and drove me to the Greyhound station in downtown Tulsa. "I've told you everything I can about your daddy," she said, nodding to the bus that sat idling in the morning light. "You want to know more, you gotta go do some of your growing up where he did his."

I remember the worrisome way she held on to me, the way she waved only once before turning away and wiping her face as the bus pulled out of the station, and I remember the way she stood there a month later, holding back tears when my bus rolled back into town, as if she'd been standing there all the while I was gone, holding her breath, afraid that if she left I might never come back. In a way, it made sense to me even as I was leaving: my father had been killed before I was born; she had to let me go, had to let me learn who he'd been. But even that morning on the bus, turned around in my seat and all mixed up in my guts — even then I had the feeling that what hurt her most was not letting me go, but having to stay behind.

She'd met my father while vacationing with her parents on the Texas coast near Matagorda Bay. He'd been down from his father's farm in Shiner for the weekend, fishing with friends, and two months later he'd driven his old Chevy truck up to Oklahoma to ask for her hand and bring her back home with him. Half a year later he left for war, four months after that he was in the ground, and she'd moved from Texas up to Tulsa where her parents lived, and where I was born.

Married less than a year before she was widowed, she couldn't have known my father all that much better than I did, and I imagine what she did know was full of holes, voids she could only dream of filling. When I think about it today, I can almost put words to that nine-year-old inkling I had swirling in my stomach the morning I left for Grandpa's. I can see my mother kissing me goodbye and putting me on the bus. I can watch her through the back window as the bus rolls away, watch her standing there, her summer dress swirling around her knees, one foot on the curb and one in the highway, not waving but watching, watching her son go south, and I know she wished she were going too. Instead, she was heading north with Stan Kittridge, the balding banker who would introduce her to his relations in Chicago, and who would marry her the next summer. Who would buy us a house on the red clay

banks of Hominy Creek and drive us to Dallas for Cow-
boys games some Sundays, and who, much to his credit,
told me I could call him Stan, just Stan, though he would
become over the years more like a father than the man he
was to me that summer—some stranger in a necktie who
never took his shoes off, who always winked at me for no
good reason, and who called my mother a peach.

Before my visit that summer, all I'd known of Grandpa
Havleck was sharp words and sharp steel. Every year since
I could remember, he'd sent me a new pocketknife for my
birthday, and though I'd handled them endlessly, pulling
out the blades and inspecting the engraving for some secret
message, all I'd ever found was the manufacturer's name
and the grade of stainless steel. When I'd ask my mother
about him, she'd frown and find something that needed
doing around the house, something to keep her hands busy
while she talked. "He's a bitter pill," she told me, "and I
don't want you thinking that's how your daddy was, 'cause
he wasn't. He was outgoing and loud sometimes, but always kind. Your Grandpa Havleck, he's all eaten up on the
insides with guilt, says one thing and feels another. Deep
down, though, he's good people. Has to be, else he couldn't
have fathered your father."

Before my trip, I was warned to expect some strange
behavior, a little ribbing here and there, a bunch of what
my mother called "macho hooey about Texas-this and
Texas-that."

What I didn't expect, even after having spent most of

August with the old man, was for him to sit me down in the porch swing out back of his farmhouse in Shiner, fish a cold bottle of Lone Star from the cooler he kept by the door, and slap it into my hand.

"There you go, boy," he said, and once he'd pried the caps off the bottles, he slipped the bottle opener into the chest pocket of his T-shirt, gave it a little pat for safekeeping, took a swig of his beer, and then shot me a look of disgusted confusion.

"Whatcha just looking at it for?" he said. "Go on, you little Okie. Drink it. That there's a Lone Star you got, and if ever there was a little Oklahoma green-ass in need of some liquid Texas, it's you."

Grandpa hiked his jeans up under the enormous hump of his belly and rubbed his head, which had been bald, he claimed, since he was nineteen and came down with scarlet fever. Four days and nights, a temperature so high the whites of his eyes went red as a July sunset, and when the fever broke he'd washed up, looked in the mirror, and run a comb through his hair for the last time. "It all come out," he'd told me one night. "All at once, four swipes of the comb and it was as gone as gone can get." Now I held my beer and marveled at him: at his head, slick and shining in the sun, a large vein snaking its blue way above one eyebrow; at his stomach, so slumped and low-slung you couldn't see his belt buckle. This was not the kind of man a boy disobeyed. This was the daddy of the daddy I'd never met, the man who, according to my mother, had walked his twenty-year-old son down to the recruiting office in Shiner as soon as the draft was reinstated. The man who told the recruiting officer, "This here's my only son, and he'd rather fight than farm. I figure if he's got to go get himself killed, he'd better damn well die a Marine." The man who, when he got word that my daddy had done just that after being taken down by friendly fire, went back to that recruiting office, slammed the purple heart my mother had gotten in the mail on that officer's desk, and told the man the Havlecks didn't have any use for a dead man's medal, so why didn't the Marines just melt it down and make some bullets and teach their boys how to shoot them straight—maybe at the enemy for a change.

In a matter of hours I would learn that these stories were more legend than history, more talk than truth, but at the time, sitting there on the porch with a bottle of beer in my hand and nine years of mystery still roped tight inside me, all I could see was an enormous frowning man. This was a man you didn't mess with, no matter what my mother said about his talk being hooey, a man who wanted me to drink what he'd given me, so I took a careful swig, and it was cold on my teeth and bitter down deep in my throat and altogether surprising the way only a boy's first beer can be.

"Now we're talkin'," he said, and after he'd polished the rest of his off with one turn of the bottle, he proceeded to inform me that even though the Spoetzl Brewery was just five miles away in downtown Shiner, and even though it was made in Texas, Shiner beer was still more Czech than Texan. They imported all the fixings, he told me, all the barley and hops and—hell, maybe even the water for all he knew. And the guy who ran the place, Walter Dudek—*Pure-D Euro-peean.* A nice enough guy, sure, but no Texan.

I took another drink, my cheeks awash with a first-beer flush, and I wondered if I was drunk already, if my increasing confusion about Grandpa was the product of good beer or bad memory. "But you're Czech," I said, "aren't you? I thought all we Havlecks were."

His face went fierce, his chapped lips parting in disbelief, the skin atop his head bunched up in distasteful furrows. "The hell I am," he said, setting his empty on the porch rail and letting loose a groan when he bent over, opening the cooler for another. "My daddy was Czech. Sure enough, no getting around it. Landed in Galveston when he was twenty-one. But me and your daddy, we're Texans, though one of us is a dead Texan. And you, boy, you're a dustbowl-loving Okie." He shook his head and bubbled his beer and made a clicking sound with his tongue. "Sorry to say it, son, but it's the God's honest truth. Your grandma, God keep her, she even dug up some dirt out here in the yard and sent it in a box up there to Tulsa so you could be born over Texas soil, and boy, I'll never know why in the hell she did it, I really won't, but she used UPS instead of Tex-Pak. Can you believe it? Got-*damn*, boy, do you know who *owns* Tex-Pak?"

I shook my head that I didn't.

"Lady Bird Johnson, that's who. We're talking Texan from titties to toenails."

Out back of the barn, Grandpa's prized bird dog, Alamo,

was raising Cain in his kennel. Grandpa hollered, "Easy, Allie," then he took me tight by the back of the neck. "Listen, boy. You hear it?"

"The dog?" I asked, wondering if maybe the old man had gone deaf the way he'd gone bald—all in an instant.

"Not the *dog*, boy. What the dog *hears*. Bobwhite quail, way out in the pasture, bobwhitin' their little feathered asses off."

I turned my ear to the south, but all I could hear was the dog howling and the buzz of mosquitoes and the almost liquid hiss of the wind swirling in the scrub grass, rattling the crippled-looking branches of the mesquite tree by the barn. I looked up at Grandpa, who still had me firm by the neck, and shook my head.

"You can't hear 'em?" he asked. "Not even a little?"

"No, sir," I said, the way my mother had taught me.

"Well," he said, smiling, "me neither. Can't hear shit, matter of fact, but that dog can. You better believe that dog can."

I laughed and took another sip of beer and Grandpa gave me a playful shake before turning me loose. "You know what, boy? It's a damn shame we didn't get that soil up there in time. You might have made an okay Texan."

I finished my beer and Grandpa pulled me another from the ice. Hard as he was to understand, and callous as he could be sometimes, I couldn't bring myself to feel much of anything but respect for him—not, anyway, with him finally smiling and giving me beer and acting like he might, somewhere in the deep-down insides of him, love me like the son he'd lost, so I asked him—I said, "That would have counted? If the soil would've been under the bed?"

The sun was going down, and Grandpa looked out west over his field of August cotton to where the sky was blistered with clouds. "Hell, boy, I ain't gonna lie to you—probably not. Probably wouldn't have made a damn bit of difference." He swiped his fingers over his bald head like he expected to find his hair grown suddenly back into place. "But I don't reckon it could have hurt."

There always were, in Grandpa's way of speaking, lessons to be learned about the way Texans did things, or didn't do them, and to me, they began that summer to sound like his way of talking about my father without speaking of him directly. The morning after I'd arrived in Texas, three weeks before Grandpa gave me my first beer, after a nighttime storm that threw hail hard against the roof and softened the soil with rain, he took me out to the dog kennel where his pointer, Alamo, was curled up in the shade. He scratched the dog on the neck and took a long look inside his floppy ears and filled the food and water bowls, all the while whispering, "That's right, Allie. Just a few more weeks and we'll put you on the birds."

Out back of the chicken shed, he reached into a burlap sack and threw feed around on the ground the way Stan dealt cards when he and my mother played gin after dinner most nights. Then Grandpa took hold of me by a belt loop and pulled me out to the pasture. "There you go," he said, spitting down to direct my attention toward a glistening pile of cow flop in the grass. "Looks like a good one to me, kiddo. Reckon you can give her a good stomp?"

I looked up at him, at the tight smile of his lips, at the thin thread of spit that still swung from the stubble on his chin. "Go on," he said. "Texans don't ever mind a little shit on their boots."

After I'd stomped around awhile, playing a crude game of hopscotch from cow patty to cow patty, Grandpa looked at my boots and laughed and said he thought that would probably do for starters. "We're going to have to teach you to use the boot jack," he said. "If she ain't haunting the place already, you better believe your grandma will be rattling chains tonight if you track that stuff through her house. She never could abide that." Grandpa pulled the neck of his T-shirt down and scratched at the skin beneath all the wiry white hairs he had growing there, his lips still working all the while, like he'd lost his voice but not the will to make words. Pulling his hand from his shirt, he looked me up and down. "She never could," he said.

"Did my daddy do that?" I asked. "Track mud in the house?"

Grandpa looked down at me and then back out toward the west. "Mud and some worse," he said, and for a long while he stood there, looking out over the pasture and cotton fields, digging around in his ear with a pinkie finger like there was something stuck in his head he couldn't dislodge. When he turned back my way, his eyes widened as if he were surprised to find me still standing there.

"What's a boot jack?" I asked.

"A boot jack, boy, is what you use when you're done working. Which we ain't."

He reached around in his pocket and threw me a set of keys. Over by the chicken shed where the old Allis-Chalmers tractor was parked, two dozen or more hens were shucking and clucking, pecking at the ground for the feed Grandpa had tossed there. "Get on up there," he said, nodding at the orange tractor. "We're fixin' to teach you to drive."

The sun was coming up in full now, and the chickens scurried around as if fueled by the heat. As I was climbing onto the tractor, my boots lost hold and I smacked my shin so soundly against the foot plate that the pain sparked and caught fire and licked its way up my leg and into my guts. My mouth flooded with spit and I thought for sure I'd be sick. "Well," Grandpa said, slapping the tractor seat with the palm of his hand, "you ain't in much danger of riding rodeos anytime soon, but this is just a tractor, for the love of God. Try her again."

Once I'd worked my way into the seat, Grandpa pulled himself up beside me, sitting on the rear-wheel fender while he taught me how to pull the choke out and count slow to ten before cranking the engine. While I sat there, squinting into the sun and feeling the machine rumble and growl beneath me, he got down with a groan and hooked up the disc plow. And then it was time to drive.

For the next hour, Grandpa sat on the fender while I drove, teaching me how to stand hard on the clutch to shift gears, how to raise and lower the implement, coaching me as I drove slowly forward, plowing under the remains of the springtime garden while the chickens bobbed and weaved all around us. "You got it," he said. "Hot damn, son, you're shittin' fire and pissin' fuel now, ain't it? You're driving."

Perched atop the tractor, with the night's rain steaming up from the ground and the musky-sweet smell of black soil washing around me, everything seemed under my power — the tractor, sputtering forward and jerking so hard when I shifted gears that it threw me forward into the steering wheel; my legs, too short and rubber-muscled though they were from standing hard on the clutch and the gas; the ground beneath me, turning over in my wake. Everything. Grandpa sat there beaming, wiping sweat from his forehead and nodding out toward the next plot of ground he wanted tilled.

Straining against the wheel, I turned us around and steered toward the unbroken earth. In front of us, a sea of chickens parted in fluttering waves and I was thinking Moses couldn't have done it any better when I stood on the clutch and felt my boot start sliding.

Either because of the shit on my soles or the wobbly way my legs were working, I slid clean off the clutch, coming down solid with my other foot on the gas. What happened next was fast and black and smelled of fuel. The engine screamed, shooting us forward while diesel-black swirled from the smokestack and the chickens came alive, taking to the air, leaving feathers aloft behind them. Grandpa grabbed the wheel and got a boot on the brake, and as he brought us to a stop it was all I could do to hang on. I clamped my eyes tight against the smoke and the sun and the world rolling by, and I wanted like hell to be anywhere but here, anywhere but on this machine with an old man I hardly knew and the father I'd come here to find just as absent as he'd always been in Oklahoma.

For years I'd been trying to force him into existence, to think of him and imagine his reaction to the skinny and timid boy I'd become. I'd tell myself he was looking down, taking note of how clumsy I was. I'd paint disapproval onto his face, convincing myself that failure and fear were what he'd come to expect from me. After all, surely he'd been watching all my life, watching me run to the school washroom to puke whenever a fight broke out, when just standing there, watching in a crowd while two boys flattened each other's noses could turn my body against me. I'd try to imagine him looking down with a frown while I shut myself up in my room on bright Oklahoma afternoons when the neighborhood was alive with baseball games and swimming pool parties. He can see you, I thought, but I never convinced myself it was true, never got phantom whiffs of his aftershave or felt him leaning over my shoulder while I played.

Instead, he'd come to me in my sleep, or I'd go to him, skimming over a dreamscape of treetops and diving into the shadows, where I'd find him flat on his back, blood bubbling from the jagged hole at his hairline. This was my father, mud-caked and silent in a swampy jungle somewhere, staring up empty-eyed at the sky. I'd slosh through the muck to find his helmet, now flecked with bone and flesh and filling with green water twenty yards away from him, carried across the swamp by the bullet some buddy of his had put through his head. This was the father I'd grown up with. A man too far gone to look down on me and frown. A man too dead, even in dreams, to be brought back to life.

Now Grandpa killed the engine and looked over his shoulder at the damage I'd done. "Looks like you just plowed us some lunch," he said.

We climbed down, walked back around the implement, and there in the broken rows of dirt was a hen with its head caved in. Grandpa took hold of its feet and held it up so I could see. It surprised me that I felt nothing inside, no bitter swirl of bile in my stomach, no desire to run until I was breathless somewhere and well hidden. No nothing. Instead, I reached out and plucked a feather from the bird, twirled it between my fingers, and let it fall to the ground. "I'm sorry," I said. "I didn't mean to."

Grandpa shoved the bird my way. He snorted and coughed and spat a wad of phlegm into the soil. "We don't talk that way in Texas," he said, "and if we gotta kill chickens all day long until that sticks in your head, we'll do it. You can't apologize for killing, boy, or for dying either. There's no sense in it. You're either too dead to say the words or too dead to hear them."

Grandpa handed me the bird and I held it away from my body while he spread the legs and plucked the feathers between them. "Get your knife out," he said.

I reached into my pocket, feigning surprise when I came

up empty. Early on, my mother had laid down the law about Grandpa's gifts, and I'd never taken one of the knives he'd sent me any farther from the house than the backyard. "I must of left it in my other jeans," I said.

"Is that a fact," he said, pulling a silver lockblade from his back pocket. "Then use this one. Cut her right down there by the vent, just slit an inch or thereabouts so you can get a couple fingers in there and sweep the guts out."

I took the knife and pulled out the blade and the sun threw sparks of light from the steel. I held it in my hand, and there, etched in the knife's silver casing, was my father's name. Something flared in me, some hot desire to do harm. I thought about the schoolyard back home, the cracked dirt playground where boys would circle each other, wiping blood from the corners of their mouths while a ring of spectators egged them on, and now the thought didn't make my stomach churn, didn't send me running, holding puke in my mouth, toward the washroom. I wanted to fight. I wanted to hear my fist crack against someone's nose, to feel the tightening ring of onlookers flex around me while I drew blood. I looked at the knife in my hand. This was what I'd been waiting for, half expecting year after year when I'd unwrapped my birthday gifts from Grandpa. The knife with *Billy H.* etched deep in its silver. The knife that belonged to me, that was mine. The knife that never came.

I ran my thumb over the etching, and when I looked up Grandpa was holding the chicken's legs apart, chewing on the inside of his cheek. "Go on," he said. "Cut."

I gripped the knife, sliding the blade into the bird's skin, inhaling as the sour and animal smell of it filled the air. Stepping back, I looked down at the slight smear of blood on the blade, then back at Grandpa. His eyes were tired, unblinking, shifting up and down from my face to the knife. He held his hand out, flexing his fingers.

I hesitated, pulling the knife close to my chest.

"You got something to say?" he said.

I wiped the blade on my jeans, snapped it closed, and handed it over.

"You sure?" he said, sliding it into his back pocket. "Texans don't mince words, you know."

What Texans did do, apparently, was put loaded shotguns in the hands of hung-over nine-year-olds. The morning after the beer, Grandpa woke me with a shake of the shoulders before dawn. "This is going to be beautiful," he said. "Get your boots on."

In the kitchen, Grandpa stood in a wide-legged stance at the stove, whistling while he fried potatoes and bacon. When I sat down at the table, he turned, nodding at the cup of coffee in front of me. "Drink it," he said. "Texans ain't ever slow with a cup of joe."

After breakfast, he took me into the den, pulled open a drawer under the gun case, and this time, when he spoke, he wasn't talking about Texans. He was talking about my father, and there was something rough and hushed in his voice. "This here was your daddy's," he said, handing me a leather hunting vest that, when I put it on, came clear down to my knees. He opened a box of shells and dumped the contents into one of the vest pockets. My head was throbbing and all that weight in one pocket threw my balance out of whack. "Don't worry about that," he said, watching me sway on my feet. "Fill the other side up with birds and you'll straighten up just fine."

Then he gave me the gun, a single-shot .28, and showed me how to break it open, how to load it, how to hold it up tight against my cheek when I fired. "It was your daddy's first gun," he said, shaking his head. "He'd of wanted you to have it, but it stays right here with me till you're sixteen, got it? There's something else, too."

I nodded, feeling the cold weight of the gun in my hands while Grandpa rifled around in the drawer. "This ain't for wearing," he said, pushing a velvet-covered box at me. Now his eyes were cast down at his boots. He cracked his knuckles one by one. I gave the thing a shake, and I must have had an uneasy smile on my face. This was the kind of box my mother kept her pearls in.

I flipped the box open and Grandpa looked hard at me. "I'm serious, now," he said. "It's bad luck to wear a dead man's medal."

It was shining, the purple ribbons smooth and unfrayed, the emblem bright with the gold profile of a man any first-grader would know, and as I stood there tracing Washington's face with my thumb, I couldn't imagine what a man from my history books could possibly have to do with my father. "This is it?" I asked. "The real one? I thought you gave it back."

Grandpa pulled his gun from the cabinet and busied

himself checking the action, breaking it open and blowing into the receiver and flipping the safety on and off. "I
should have," he said. "I wanted to. Couldn't bring myself
to do it, is all. Couldn't bring myself to part with it at all
until now." He leaned his gun against the wall and put his
callused hand against my cheek. "I'm sorry, kiddo. I am,
okay? Tell your mother I said so."

Outside, the wind had blown its way by overnight. The
cotton stalks stood stiff in the fields and the sun was just
hinting over the horizon. Already it was hot. Grandpa let
Alamo out of his kennel and leashed him up on the end
of a rope. The dog looked up at us, raised his haunches
high, stretching his forelegs out in front of him as if to
give us a better view of the chocolate brown splotches on
his hindquarters. His ears twitched forward and Grandpa
said, "That's right, Allie. We're going to work." Handing
me his gun, he bent forward with a groan and gave Alamo a
two-handed scratching around the neck. The dog yawned
and licked Grandpa's wrists, then rolled his head around to
make sure Grandpa didn't miss a spot. "Best gun dog there
is," Grandpa said. "English pointers, they call 'em, but just
look at that dog. Ain't he a beauty? English, my ass. He was
whelped just down the highway a stretch in Yoakum."
      In the southern pasture, we walked until we met the
barbed-wire fence that separated Grandpa's land from
the neighbor's cornfield. "We'll work the fence line until
an hour after sunup," Grandpa said, spitting between his
teeth. "They're hiding out here, but when the day breaks

they're gonna want to eat, and boy, let me tell you, we're gonna feed them something no living thing ever gets hungry enough to swallow."

Alamo kept lurching against the rope, and when Grandpa let him go, I knew I'd been told the truth about him. This was a dog that knew what to do with some acreage. He worked the field just the way Grandpa had said he would. While we walked straight along the fence, the dog ran, quartering back and forth, working fifty yards or so out before turning back toward the fence line, zigzagging in a set pattern just ahead of us. For every yard we covered, he covered twenty, and when he turned, stopping suddenly and leaning into a point maybe forty yards from us, his tail gone rigid and curved and held high in the air, Grandpa made a clicking sound with his tongue and began walking toward him.

Grandpa whoaed the dog and kicked around in the pasture grass, and the birds—two of them—flushed fast and loud and low toward the glare of daybreak in the east. Grandpa let out a little laugh, like he'd seen this trick before, then peppered the horizon with shot.

I turned, leaning forward into the gun, and in that instant I imagined what it must have been like to be my father. A man with mud on his boots and the tickle of ragweed in his nose, the smooth and solid cool of a walnut stock against his cheek. A man comfortable with a gun in his hands, here at home or anywhere else, by damn. A man, through and through, dead or alive, and here I was, his son, but something was locked tight inside, rusted shut, and when that bird quartered south and out of range, there was nothing I could do but stand there looking down the barrel, my finger limp on the trigger.

Grandpa broke his gun open, ejecting the spent shell. He looked down at Alamo, who was holding point, head held high to mark the fallen bird.

"Dead bird," Grandpa said. Alamo turned to me with what seemed a look of contempt in his tired bird-dog eyes, then broke out to retrieve the kill. Grandpa let out a sad whistle, a note held long and sliding low. The sound of a make-believe bomb dropping from the sky. He traded guns with me, broke mine open, and held the shell maybe four inches from my face.

"What the hell is this?" he said, making the same disgusted face he had the day before when I'd looked at my beer too long before tilting it back. "Boy, no matter how many times you load this thing in that gun, it ain't ever gonna shoot itself." He slid the shell back into my gun. "What happened?"

I could tell by the abrupt way he handed the gun over to me that he knew the answer, knew it even before I did. I'd been scared. Scared to shoot, sure, but mostly scared to miss. But when he frowned and narrowed his eyes in on me, I knew he still expected an answer, and fear, I realized, wasn't half as bad as what I felt now—small and fumbling and not at all like the son Grandpa must have remembered.

"I've never shot one before," I said.

"Well hell, boy, it's not any harder than pissing in a pond.

Just point and shoot, that's all. Go on, then. Give it a try so you get the feel of it."

I don't know what I expected, but when I raised that gun to my shoulder and pressed my cheek up tight to its smooth, finished stock, I felt almost at home with myself. I imagined some invisible enemy in the sky, some war I'd never been a part of before. I saw my daddy beside me, sighting in his weapon, and I swung the gun through the morning air, tracing a cloud with the barrel.

With the bird gripped softly in his mouth, Alamo came busting back through the brush.

"Go on," Grandpa told me, and when I squeezed the trigger, in my mind, I was strong and meant to be that way and I was killing nothing and everything all at once. I was killing, and there wasn't anything that could stop me. Not the recoil slamming my shoulder, not the blast ringing sharp in my ears. When Grandpa pulled his bird from Alamo's mouth, I broke the gun open, shoved another shell into the receiver, and when I looked up Grandpa was nodding, casting the dog back out to hunt, making that sound with his tongue before giving me a wink.

He reloaded and fell in behind the dog. I followed, taking note of the slight bulge of my daddy's knife in his back pocket. I knew then that there were things that would always be kept from me, things I'd never know. Still I walked on, determined now that the hollow twinge of loss in my chest was something I could learn to carry, and bear, a medal of manhood I'd make myself strong enough to wear.

Today when I think of that morning, of the scrub grass crunching beneath my boots and the weight of my father's vest heavy on my shoulders, of the worn, gamy smell of dried blood and leather, I know that as I walked that field I began to imagine myself as a man. I know it as surely as I know now I was fooling myself, propping myself up against the wide field of emptiness I'd found in place of all the answers I'd expected Texas would hold. But still, there I was, nine years old and proud, beer bile and coffee swirling in my nerve-cinched stomach. Nine years old and about to lay waste to some bobwhite quail. Nine years old and sweating just after dawn and long of nine-year-old stride, and strong. I imagined stepping off that bus in a few weeks, the recognition on my mother's face when she saw me in that vest, the Purple Heart pinned to my chest. She'd wear an open-lipped look of surprise, put her hands on my shoulders as she marveled at who and what I'd become. She'd smile a smile I'd never seen before except in photographs of her with my father. I would be a man. A man, by damn, and that was the hope I was holding on to the next time I pulled the trigger.

When Alamo went staunch with point, Grandpa approached from the side, said, "Whoa, there. Whoa, boy. Whoa, that's right," and when he kicked in front of the dog, a whole covey came shooting and screeching and in all directions from the grass. A half dozen of them, at least. Grandpa said, "Lord a-mighty," and got off a shot. Alamo broke point and gave chase, and when I swung my gun I was alive with adrenaline, my toes curling in my boots, and the pair of birds I'd sighted in were skimming only a couple feet off the ground with Alamo running right in their wake. Too close, too close, I knew, but then I saw that dog's face, the accusing look he'd given me earlier. I imagined the whistling sound that Grandpa had made, and when the bomb hit the ground in my mind, I squeezed the trigger.

It happened just like that, that fast, no slow motion like you see at the movies when something dies. The dog, by the time we got up to it, was bleeding and lying still and breathing, but not from its mouth. I stood back while Grandpa knelt beside him. I stood and listened to the whisper-slick sound of a dying dog sucking air through a hole in its lung.

"Mercy," Grandpa said, clamping his hand over the wound. "He's in shock. Jesus, boy. Give me that vest."

I took a step back, jammed my hands into the vest pockets. "I can't," I said, "I'm sorry," because in a way I was, and because there wasn't anything else I could think of to say.

Grandpa leaned close to the dog, pressing down, blood rising up between his fingers. "We don't talk that way here," he said, looking up. His eyes were electric, flashing with sunlit tears. Pulling a hand from the dog, he punched the hard ground with his fist. "I already told you that, boy. Now give me that goddamn vest."

"I'm sorry," I said again, because my feet had gone numb in my boots and the dog wouldn't stop dying and I suddenly didn't care how Texans talked. Besides, he wasn't talking about Texans. I knew he wasn't. He was talking about my daddy. He was talking about my daddy and he was talking about me, and I wasn't sorry just for killing his dog. I was sorry because I couldn't do what he asked, what he thought a man should do, couldn't bring myself to take off that vest. I didn't want him to wrap it around that dog. I didn't want the dog bleeding on it. I wanted to wear it home and see that bright look of recognition in my mother's eyes. I wanted to take it to school and show my friends and tell them who once had worn it.

The dog was shivering, staring blank-eyed at the wide morning sky and Grandpa was crying in earnest now, pounding the earth with a bloody fist and cursing God and saying, "Easy Allie, easy old boy, I got you baby, I got you now," and I was just standing there, holding my own, wishing like hell I was back in Oklahoma where I knew now I belonged. I worked my boot around in the soil and I wished myself gone, wished the dog alive, and then I took a step forward and stopped wishing things that couldn't come true, things I couldn't force into being any more than I could bring my father back to life in my dreams. I took another step and put my gun on the ground and knelt down beside my Grandpa while he smoothed Alamo's fur, and I stayed there with him awhile, helping him help his dog die.

The Only Good Thing I've Heard

THE BABY HAD died inside her, and Tammy hadn't been out of bed in five days, not since the doctor induced labor that Saturday. Raymond had taken Monday and Tuesday off, spent the afternoons making soup from Tammy's recipes, flipping through old magazines and doing laundry, matching socks. He ironed his blue hospital scrubs, knowing they looked fine pulled straight from the dryer. He paced the small rooms of their apartment, going from small task to small task, unable to sit still and unwilling to hold any one thing too long in his hands. Taking the remote control from the coffee table, he'd set it next to him on the couch without turning on the TV. He'd even set out to disassemble the baby's changing table that Tammy had gotten through mail order. He'd twisted a wing nut from the aluminum support at the base, and that was it. He'd stopped there. He remembered working as a teenager in the nursery at St. Jude, his parents' church in Houston. The other babysitters had called him Diaper Boy because he hadn't minded the changing, because he'd liked the smell of powder and the crinkling sound of disposable diapers, the milky, cooing thank-yous of freshly changed babies.

On Sunday he called Marcelo's, the restaurant near Lake Austin where Tammy had been sous-chef for five years, ever since graduating from culinary school the year they were married. Raymond spoke in a low, deliberate voice, one he'd been forcing from the back of his throat for days. "She'll be back," he told the manager. "Hopefully soon."

Twice a day he gave Tammy the pills Dr. Rusk had prescribed to help her sleep. He filled two glasses with filtered water and pretended, as he might have done with a child, to take a pill himself, and they drank the water in unison, staring at each other with unblinking eyes over the rims of the glasses. From a chair by the bed, without touching her, he'd watch her sleep, often for hours at a time, her long hair thrown above her head, lost between the mattress and the wall.

On Thursday morning, his second day back at work, Raymond cursed the elevator when it stopped on the fourth floor. The doors slid open and a man with chapped lips and a double-breasted suit stepped in from the maternity ward. Raymond kept his eyes lowered, fixed on the laces of his white Reeboks. "It's going up," he said.

"Fair enough," the man said. He swung his arms lightly

at his sides, rocking on the balls of his feet, and Raymond bit down on the inside of his cheek. They act like that, he thought. Like they can't wait for a day or two to pass so they can wrap them in blankets and drive them to some nice little house, maybe up by Lake Travis. Lay them face-down on their stomachs in the new crib and stand for hours in the remodeled nursery watching them sleep, smiling stupidly and inhaling the smells of baby powder and new pink paint.

"Don't mind at all," the man said. "I'll take the roundtrip." He smiled and Raymond noticed one tooth, up top. Crooked. The others were straight and dull, but white. He knew it was senseless, but Raymond took a certain pleasure in locating the man's hidden imperfection. "Just fine by me," the man said.

Raymond got off on the seventh floor. The man said, "Take care." He was leaning on the back wall of the elevator, and Raymond nodded without looking back. When the doors slid shut, the man was whistling.

After signing in and rolling his cart from the storage closet, Raymond walked his rounds. There were only three patients on the wing, and the thought of Melody, the little girl in the room closest to the nurses' station, turned Raymond toward the far end of the hall. The girl was five, covered from the waist down with third-degree burns from a water heater explosion. With burns, Raymond had learned, oral medication, even narcotics, didn't make much of a dent in the pain, and topical ointments prevented the wounds from breathing, so it was Raymond's job to hold the girl still while she screamed, to force her waist deep into the debridement whirlpool while the water and Dr. Dutch worked the dead skin free from the wounds. Yesterday, after her treatment, the whirlpool had bubbled with sickeningly pink water.

As Raymond rolled his cart down the hall, nurses waved to him shyly from their center station, forcing tight-lipped smiles. They had sent a sympathy card with a Bible verse on the cover: *And this is the promise he hath promised us, even eternal life.* There were signatures inside, some that Raymond didn't even recognize. He'd worried about them, wondering how these names had escaped him. Early on, he'd made a point of meeting the other hospital employees, from the radiology staff to the cafeteria cooks; even the doctors waved, gave him the thumbs-up sign when they passed him in the halls. They liked the way he joked with the patients, the way he never pretended to be more than a nurse's aid, and then suddenly, a month before, after three years on the evening shift, he'd been moved up to days on the burn unit. Normally the unit was staffed only by RNs and LVNs, and Raymond was proud of the move. Three-fifty more an hour, and while he thought—at least most of the time—that he'd earned the promotion, Raymond wondered now if it was just another symptom of downsizing. As he wheeled the cart into Mrs. Lane's room, he was thinking it was all the same.

Mrs. Lane's bottom lip was burned mostly away, and Raymond tried not to imagine it melting, dripping down onto her chin. He was surprised she could still talk, but she spoke without squinting or slurring her words—without even the slightest sign of pain. The day before, while Dr. Dutch and Nurse Taylor peeled the loose burned skin from the old woman's chin with tweezers and scissors, scouring the raw flesh clean with a pad that looked like the one Tammy used on her baking dishes, Raymond had held the woman around the waist, keeping her bent above the whirlpool, whispering in her ear, as she screamed for them to stop, that it was almost over.

Hers had been the first debridement therapy of the day, and it was too much for him: the sight of bloody new skin and thick yellow pus and the smell of old singed flesh, and afterward he'd walked inconspicuously to the restroom and vomited.

Now Mrs. Lane sat tilted up in her bed as if nothing had happened.

"Hey, good lookin'," Raymond said, moving to the bed. At the top of her neck, folds of loose skin bunched beneath a large square bandage that curved from under her lips down over her chin. Raymond touched her arm, pulled the blankets tight around her narrow hips. The TV was going in the corner near the ceiling. *Wheel of Fortune.*

"Might need some help with this one," Mrs. Lane said, nodding at the game show's wall of unturned blocks. "I'm thinking *Babes in Toyland.*"

"Don't know, Mrs. Lane," Raymond said. "Says they're looking for historical people."

"Well, I'm not *blind.* You don't think the babes count?"

Mrs. Lane raised a hand to her bandaged chin, tracing the smooth adhesive edges with her bony fingers and frowning. On the bedstand, beside a crumpled apple juice box, a picture of a young woman and three boys in matching suits faced the bed.

"Handsome family there," Raymond said.

"Oh, yes," she said. "That's my favorite, from back when Charlie was still alive. He hated me dressing the boys like that, but he let me all the same. He took it—the picture, I mean."

"Quite a group," Raymond said. He crossed the room and parted the drapes. Outside, the sun threw the shadow of the building onto the parking lot below. Two nurses stood talking in the shade beside an old pickup, and a line of cars sat waiting at the light on Lamar. "Look at that. Springtime in Austin, Mrs. Lane, and you got the best seat in the house."

Raymond turned and the woman was scratching her neck at the edge of the bandage. The day before, Nurse Taylor had told Raymond how it happened, how the old woman, in what the nurse called a "state of confusion," had tried to eat a spoonful of hot bacon grease. "Believe that?" Nurse Taylor had said. "And she seems so on top of things. Best keep a special eye on her."

"Go easy on that bandage, Mrs. Lane," Raymond said. "Gotta give that burn a chance to heal up. Look out there. You got a perfect view of the capitol building from right there in bed."

"Can't say as I care much about the capitol," she said.

She ran her hands up and back on her lap, shaping the blankets around the tops of her legs. "My boys are all gone now," she said. "Two in Dallas and the other in Tulsa. Kids of their own, except for Charlie Junior."

In the parking lot, the two nurses climbed into separate cars.

"He's coming to visit," Mrs. Lane said. "Charlie Junior is. Driving all the way down here tomorrow after work." She touched the picture frame, running a finger across the top. "We're all done with those treatments," she said, rubbing her thighs with cupped hands. "Aren't we, Raymond?"

All at once his feet grew hot, burning in his shoes. He crossed the room and pressed the bed switch to sit her up straight. When he'd signed in, Dr. Dutch's schedule for the day was posted at the nurses' station; Mrs. Lane's name was near the top. "I'm not sure," he said.

The bed's electric motor whined and Raymond remembered the muscles clenching in her stomach, the tight flexing against his arm as he held her forward over the water and went tense himself, gritting his teeth against the echo of her hoarse cries between the concrete walls. Raymond took a quick breath and looked into the hall as if—what? Afraid to be caught stealing air? Leaving the room, he remembered the whirlpool, the sound of water swirling beneath them while he held the old woman in place.

The Friday before, Raymond had sat at the foot of the bed rubbing Tammy's feet after she sat up abruptly and turned on the lamp. She was seven months pregnant, her feet were swollen, red as if blistered, and she'd been jolted awake by the feeling that something within her had changed.

"Something stopped," she said, her eyes blinking in the sudden light of their bedroom. She said it over and over — "It feels like something just stopped" — and Raymond worked the arches of her feet with his thumbs. It was late, nearly three, and he'd only been home a few hours after working a double shift.

"Don't get yourself excited," he said. "We're supposed to keep your blood pressure down. Have you been taking those vitamins?"

"When I can get them down. You've seen them, Ray. Horse pills. They make me gag."

"Well, then, maybe you're just deficient is all."

"You don't understand," Tammy said. "This is different. Something's not right."

The rest of the night Raymond spent trying to coax her to sleep. He warmed milk and rubbed her poor, swollen toes and turned the light back off. But even in the dark he could sense that she was awake, her blue eyes streaked with the jagged red lines of panic, and after a while he gave up. He got under the sheets and pulled her head onto his chest. He pulled her nightshirt up over her waist and traced by memory his finger between the little moles on her back. He kissed her forehead and rocked her gently on his chest. "Any better?" he asked.

She was shaking, her legs moving uncomfortably against his, pulling his hairs as she kicked and tossed. "No, Raymond," and she dug her fingernails into his chest while he held her, rocking slowly.

"What do you want to do?" he asked. He kept his voice low, struggling to be patient. Because they'd been short staffed at the hospital, with the exception of a brief break between shifts, he'd been on his feet for sixteen hours straight. When he'd gotten home, he'd fallen to dreaming easily, his body limp with exhaustion, his limbs filled with the dense, liquid weight of sleep, but now pressure was building in his chest and his lower back arched with spasms. A muscle twitched in his neck. "Well, you wanna go rushing off to the emergency room because you had a bad dream or something?"

Tammy swung her legs from the bed and shut herself up in the bathroom. "I'm awake," she said. "And it's not a dream. You don't know what the hell you're talking about, Raymond."

From under the door, a thin wedge of light spilled onto the bedroom carpet. Raymond hit his pillow and rolled to his side, but he knew he wouldn't sleep. He kept picturing Tammy as she was before the pregnancy, her dark hair spilling down to the narrow of her back, the way she cradled his head between her breasts and the fronts of her thighs when he tickled her, dipping his tongue into her navel. Two more months, he thought. The toilet flushed. Two more months and she'll be back to normal.

He got out of bed and leaned against the bathroom door. "Tammy?" he said. "Honey? I'm sorry, honey. Are you all right?"

"No, I'm not, Raymond! What have I been telling you?" She swung the door open and rested her hands on his waist. The air conditioner had kicked on and he felt the cool push of air from the vents. Tammy's cheeks were damp and flushed, her lips twisted into a terrible frown. Raymond pulled her head to his chest. He remembered the night of his twenty-fifth birthday, just a year after their wedding, when he'd been up all night with the flu. She had kept cool washcloths on his forehead and held him this way, his head on her chest, while his fever broke. And now? Now when she had been frightened from sleep?

Raymond put his lips to her ear, whispered, "You're gonna be just fine." She tilted her head back and her tongue split through her pasty lips. Her head dropped back into him, and Raymond felt the heat of her cheek soaking into his chest, sinking deep and expanding beneath the skin. He pulled her hair away from her neck and blew cool breath down her back. The tight hump of her belly pushed against his waist and he reached under her nightshirt, moving his fingers in slow, careful circles around her distended navel.

"That feel good?" he asked, and she nodded. "Okay, then," he said, and for a while, until morning, everything felt as it should.

Raymond guessed that Terence was nineteen, maybe twenty. A University of Texas cap was pushed up on his forehead, his hands raised like a surgeon awaiting gloves, wrapped and splinted from the elbows up. He smiled when Raymond filled the plastic tray with water and wrung the sponge. "No offense," he said, "but I been waiting for this and you're not exactly what I had in mind."

"You'll get over it," Raymond said, pulling the Velcro strips of Terence's gown apart at his shoulders. "We can't have you getting too excited."

Raymond worked the sponge down the boy's hairless chest, over his sternum and down onto his taut stomach. "Good to see you're awake, at least." The day before, in debridement, Raymond had struggled to keep Terence in place, his hands clasped in front of the boy's slight chest, his arms strung under Terence's stretched armpits while Doctor Dutch unwound the bandages. When the tweezers pulled a wide black layer of skin from his palm, Terence had turned his head back toward Raymond, a wet rage in his eyes. He hadn't said a word, too proud for even a whimper, and as the doctor scrubbed the backs of his raw hands, he'd passed out in Raymond's arms.

"It's the best way to go, I think," Terence said. "Wake up and it's all over."

"Might be," said Raymond. "Lean forward for me."

As Raymond washed the boy's narrow back, he worked the sponge slowly, tracing down the tight brown ridge of the kid's spine.

Before they'd married, on a scorching Saturday afternoon at Barton Springs, Raymond had watched three young boys playing in the cold water while he rubbed lotion into Tammy's back. The boys were splashing each other, karate chopping the water, slapping up arcing waves that glimmered in the sun as they fell. Raymond held thumbs on each side of Tammy's spine, counted the verte-brae as he slid his hands down toward her waist. She was so dark, shining with oil, that when Raymond circled her little moles with his thumbs—the one just under her shoulder blade, another down low on the rise of her hips—he found he was squinting. You're blinding me, he thought, and as he slid his fingers down her skin, watching the lightened trails fill in with the dark shade of blood behind tanned skin, she let out a soft, girlish moan under his weight. "I'm keeping you," she said.

After he finished, Raymond secured the Velcro holds at the shoulders of Terence's hospital gown. "Heard you got in a fight with a bonfire," he said.

Terence leaned back, his ball cap fallen over his eyes. Raymond righted it, pushing it back high on his forehead, and Terence smiled up at him. "Pretty stupid, huh?"

"Depends. What's your excuse?"

"No excuse, just a Fiji party. Lots of beer and food and some real honeys, Thetas most of 'em, and the fire, of course. Me and my pledge brother Andy were just goofing off, pushing each other around after he knocked a beer outta my hand." Terence lifted his elbows off the bed tray, frowned at the fingers curled toward his palms in their splints. "I just tripped, I don't know. Fell backward over the logs they had circled around the fire. Went to catch myself and planted my hands right in the coals. Next thing I know I'm in the back of this truck and I hear Andy screaming at the driver to go faster." Raymond wanted to speak, to assure the kid that he understood, but Terence was looking at his hands, shaking his head, and Raymond, managing only a slow nod, felt a pinch of inadequacy in his throat. As a teenager, after Hurricane Alicia had downed trees and power lines as far inland as his parents' house in Houston, Raymond remembered reaching across the kitchen table for the chimney of the lit hurricane lamp. He hadn't been thinking, meaning only to blow it out, but the rush of adrenaline clenched his fingers around the hot glass, and the white blisters rose even as he held his hand under cold tap water. It's not the same, he thought. The blisters had healed in a matter of days.

"I'm looking up at the moon," Terence said. "I'm thinking—just like a little kid, ya know—thinking it's following us, and there's this Theta with pigtails holding my head in her lap. She's looking down at me and almost crying, her eyes all wet and blue and she's saying to hold on. That's all I remember, her saying 'hold on' and my hands almost numb, not like a regular burn, where you touch a hot plate or something? More like my bones were baking under the skin."

Sitting on the foot of the bed, Raymond remembered the creaking of the rocking chair in the church nursery where he'd worked, the angry cries of a colicky infant he'd rocked for hours, her stomach tight against his chest. Even when she slept, Raymond thought, she seemed restless, squirming in his arms or under the cotton blankets in the crib. She'd looked healthy, her arms and legs fat and pink, but she couldn't lie still. She was always moving, her little stomach knotted inside her, cinched with spasms, refusing even in sleep to turn her loose.

"I tried to stay awake," Terence was saying. "I wanted to keep looking at her, but I kept passing out. Whenever the truck would hit a bump or brake real hard, I'd jolt awake, and I'd try to keep my eyes open. Tried hard so I could keep looking up at her, like if I closed them she'd disappear."

"Sounds like the perfect date for your next house party," Raymond said. "You'd be surprised. Sympathy dates." Even while speaking, smiling down at Terence, Raymond was imagining the girl in the pickup, her pigtails streaming behind her on some country road outside of town, the look on her face fading, growing lighter, translucent, then gone. Fading until the only thing looking down on him was the moon.

"She hasn't called," the boy said. "Don't even know her name."

"You will," Raymond said, but his mouth had grown dry, his tongue heavy and thick. He pictured the look on Tammy's face in those few minutes before they took the child away, when the nurse had held the blanket at her side before handing it, hesitantly, to Raymond. He'd been watching his wife. She was flushed, her face beaded with sweat, and though she knew the child was dead—had been told hours before—Raymond recognized her expressions: the raised brows, the muscles twitching in her long neck, the sad hint of hope in her parted lips. He remembered thinking the whole ugly world had gone silent, feeling a thankful leap in his stomach when Tammy screamed. "Aren't you even going to wash her! Clean her off, goddammit! Why don't you wash her off?" It was then, through the furious white echo of Tammy's voice, that he first knew that their nameless baby, colored with only the slightest cold tint of blue, had been a girl.

Before Raymond rolled his cart from the room, Terence asked him if he wouldn't mind coming back after lunch. "My mom's coming for a while, but she won't stay that long. So would you come by? I need kind of a favor."

Raymond gripped the cart's handle. "Sure thing," he said.

After lunch, Raymond waited for the nurses' lounge to clear out, and then he called. He propped his elbows on the cool Formica tabletop, held the phone tight against his ear.

When Tammy answered, her voice pulled low with the weight of drugs, he said, "Are you okay, honey?" There was breathing, the static *whish* of amplified air.

"Sleepy," she said. "My knees ache."

"That's the sedatives. Maybe we should try a day without it."

"Maybe, if you think. Would you stay home, then?"

Raymond thought of the apartment, of the way he'd paced the rooms and sat for helpless hours watching Tammy sleep. "Honey," he said. "You know I have to work."

"I know," she said. "But it's too quiet. You're the only

good thing I've heard all day—you and the yard men doing the grass. You can tell the mowers from the weedeater,
even from inside. And the blower, I think it was a blower."

"I'll be home in a few hours. You have the number, right?
By the phone?" Papers or sheets, something crisp, rustled
on the other end.

"I've got it," Tammy said. Raymond could hear her voice
rising up to its normal pitch. He wanted to know she was
all right, still his. He wanted to hear her say it, to hear *I'm
keeping you*, to know she was awake and curled under the
pile of blankets she insisted upon even in summer. He'd
shudder, he thought. His scalp would tingle at the way her
voice dipped low on *keeping*. On the back of his neck, little
hairs would rise, and everything would be like always.

"Is she still there?" she asked. "Have you seen her?"

"Honey," he said, gripping the phone and sitting back so
he could breathe.

"The baby? Have you seen my baby?"

"You know I haven't. She's at the funeral home.
Remember?"

Something was moving inside him, pushing itself forward, and he felt it all coming up, bitter and liquid in the
back of his throat: the warmth and tightness of her pregnant stomach pressed under his rib cage in bed; later, in
the hospital, her lips twisted with induced contractions,
the blue web of stilled veins under his daughter's eyes.
He swallowed, but his saliva had grown old and thick. He
stood up, picturing rippled water, oil beaded on skin, until

he knew he could keep it all down. "We can get her when you're ready," he said. "Her ashes."

"I know, Ray. I just thought—I mean, I keep dreaming and there she is, you know? I just thought we could hold her, honey. One more time, maybe. I don't know, Ray. I just wanted to—"

And now Raymond knew she was crying, knew by the sudden dip in her voice and the short breaths between words.

"It's okay," he said, sitting back at the table. He felt suddenly calm, and he realized he'd been waiting to hear her cry, to have her sit up in bed, finally lucid, and get some more of it out. He remembered the way she kept turning her head toward the fetal monitor that Saturday, holding his hand and giving it a little squeeze whenever she imagined something had moved. But Dr. Rusk had known, almost instantly, from the moment he applied the sensors to her swollen stomach. And Raymond knew too, from the doctor's look of failure, the drop of his eyes to the floor when the monitor, instead of pulsing to life, had remained motionless, a narrow blue line cutting straight across the black screen. Still, Tammy hadn't cried—not when Dr. Rusk explained how rare these things were, a cord winding so tight around an unborn throat so late in the term; not when he gave them the option of c-section; not during his careful suggestion, his warning that a cesarean could complicate natural births in the future. No, the tears had come later, with Tammy's uncontrollable shivering and the fierce grip of her hands and the decision cried out in the rising voice of a frightened child. Her head shook in short jerky swipes back and forth, and her eyes looked strangely intense — sharp, with too much white around the edges.

Now, on the phone, her voice was hushed and broken, and Raymond leaned hard into the receiver, wanting to be there, to feel her breath swirling inside his ear. "You're okay," he said, and he knew, for the first time in days, that if she wasn't, she would be.

"And you, honey," she said. "How are *you?*"

After Mrs. Lane's debridement, Raymond went to the restroom and washed his face. The woman had done better this time, no screaming. "Can you believe it?" she'd said. "Kings of England? That puzzle on *Wheel of Fortune*—what kind of silliness is that?" And when Dr. Dutch asked Raymond how he was holding up, Nurse Taylor tilted her head and said, "Raymond, we just feel terrible," and Mrs. Lane had put both hands on the arms Raymond held around her waist. Now, Raymond dried his face with paper towels and hit the oversized button on the electric dryer, standing in front of it, listening gratefully to the motor whine, letting the hot air blow under the collar of his scrubs.

In the little girl's room, Melody's mother was helping her daughter with a cardboard puzzle. Raymond stopped in the doorway. The girl's legs were bandaged completely, wrapped in stiff white up to the waist. Her dark hair was a mop of tangled curls. Before she saw him, she snapped a puzzle piece into place and applauded herself. She looked up at her mother, followed her eyes to the doorway, and reached forward with both arms, screaming. "Mommy! *No, Mommy!*" Raymond caught the woman's eyes, pointed at his watch and mouthed, "*Sorry* . . . Thirty minutes."

Terence was upright in bed, watching TV. His baseball cap sat on the tray table and his short hair was molded into a rumpled crown. "You ready for me?" Raymond asked.

Terence extended his arms, palms up, and pressed his lips together, exhaling audibly through his nose. "I don't know. You ready for me?"

"We could play this game all day, I guess," Raymond said, sitting on the edge of the bed. "And really, it'd suit me fine, but why don't you cut to the chase and try me."

"Well, how's this? I haven't taken a crap in two days."

"That's direct enough, I guess. Did you tell the nurse? I'm sure they could give you something to—"

"It's not *that*. I mean, I *need* to go." He raised his arms and the curved splints shaped his hands into claws. Talons. "I just can't ask my mom, you know? Or one of the nurses? I'm twenty years old, for chrissakes. It wouldn't be right." He dropped his hands to the sheets. "Look, I'm not having some woman wipe my ass, okay?"

Raymond smiled as he stood, holding an arm toward the adjoining bathroom. "Okay by me," he said. "But make it a good one, my friend. I know those nurses. We make this a habit and rumors will fly around this place."

Laughing, Terence swung his legs out of bed and walked stiffly into the bathroom. It was surprising, but the kid didn't seem embarrassed when Raymond lifted his gown and pulled his boxer shorts down. Once, when he'd worked evenings, Raymond had helped a nurse insert a catheter in an elderly man the night before his bypass. Raymond held the man's withered penis while the nurse inserted the tube, and the old guy wouldn't stop talking. He kept apologizing, going on and on about how it used to be bigger. But Terence didn't flinch. He waited until Raymond was done with the boxers and he lowered himself slowly.

"I can handle this next part," he said, and Raymond smiled, closing the door behind him.

While he waited, Raymond smoothed the sheets on the bed, tucked them in on the edges. He paced the room and pulled open the drapes, watched the traffic on Lamar and the steam rising from the asphalt parking lot below. He turned the TV off, then on again—Jerry Springer was shaking his head, the audience jeering at a teenage girl with pink hair and black lipstick. When Terence called from the bathroom, swinging the door open, Raymond closed the drapes.

"Sorry about this," Terence said, leaning forward.

"Oh, well," Raymond said. "No reason to be sorry. It could be worse."

"Yeah? Not much."

Raymond gripped the boy's left shoulder and moved the wadded paper down between his buttocks. As he continued, pulling paper from the roll on the wall and feeling Terence's muscles tense when a thumb grazed his skin, Raymond felt something jump in his stomach, a flutter so warm and abrupt that he almost laughed. Or cried—he couldn't tell which, but his eyes itched with the rise of tears and his toes curled in his shoes, and when he was finished, after he'd helped Terence up with his boxers and flushed the toilet and gave him a hand getting back into bed, Raymond stood still near the door, looking around the room.

"Those drapes okay?" he said.

Terence turned his head, then looked back at the door. "They're fine," he said.

"Okay then, mission accomplished, I guess."

A short woman with blue eyeshadow and black pinned-up curls stood with a tray of food behind Raymond in the doorway. "Me-meep," she said, and Raymond stepped out of her way. "That roadrunner, he kills me." She smiled and strolled to the far side of the bed. "Here you go, partner. And from what this card says, I get to feed you, too." She set the food on the table tray and smoothed her blue smock.

Terence winked at Raymond. "Out with the old and in with the new, I guess."

"Looks that way," Raymond said, but he thought of his child—*in with the new*—and he couldn't bring himself to smile.

Melody was screaming, throwing her head back and forth and clinging to her mother's neck as Nurse Taylor and Raymond lifted her onto the padded stretcher. They wheeled her slowly to the door, and in the hallway the screams bounced fierce and high off the antiseptic walls. Mrs. Lane stood outside her door with her arms folded tightly across her chest, her jaw set tight with resentment. From their station, the nurses filed charts and shuffled papers, trying not to look as Melody kicked the stretcher with her bandaged legs, clawing wildly at Raymond's arms and pulling her mother's hair. Dr. Dutch turned from the doorway and walked slowly into the debridement room as they approached, and when they wheeled her in, the girl grabbed the doorjamb, and for a few seconds everything stopped.

She looked at Raymond, her face wet, flushed with panic, her mouth open, waiting. Raymond reached toward the door and met her mother's hand on the child's arms. The back of her hand was moist and he held it, covering it softly with his palm. He wanted the woman to let him do it, to let him be the bad guy, the monster who pried the girl's hands from the wall, but the woman wouldn't let go. Melody watched them, her arms outstretched, fingernails digging into white paint, and Raymond stood looking at the woman, his pulse wild in his wrists, everything else as quiet and still as the ICU waiting room at midnight. It was a silence he recognized. White lights, the steps of the nurses' padded soles on the delivery room floor, something metal shining in the doctor's wet hands. Their daughter smeared in the white film of birth, the cord cut, now limp and harmless on her wrinkled stomach. And not a fucking sound. Just the nurse with the blanket and uncertain eyes. And then he's holding her, touching the cool, slick skin of her cheek, tracing the web of blue veins under her eyes, and Tammy is reaching out, looking up, her hands meeting his on the tiny, sunken chest of their child. The nurses just stand there, staring, another sad day's work. Then Tammy is screaming: *Aren't you even going to wash her!*

Raymond imagined tiny blue fingers reaching up in the liquid swirl of the womb, grasping overhead in the dark, unable to take hold of the cord, and now he pulled hard, prying Melody's fingers from the door and holding her wrists together in one hand. Her mother stepped back, arms at her sides. The girl was screaming again, rearing back, unable to free herself, and Raymond's ears were ablaze, thumping inside with the noise and the rage of it all. Dr. Dutch cut the bandages from her legs, his thick fingers pinched in the rings of the scissors. "I hate you," she shouted, her voice raw, but strong. Nurse Taylor was flinching, moving back from the stretcher while Raymond, a strange calm settling in his stomach, held Melody under the arms, lifting.

His hands cupping her ribs, Raymond felt the swell of her lungs, the contraction of her chest pushing the words into the room—"*I hate you!*"—and he thought he could hold her like this forever. He loved her. When he lowered her into the water, Raymond knew that he loved her, hoped she would scream until plaster fell from the walls, until silence no longer seemed possible. Go on, he thought. Let it out, goddammit. Scream.

An Instance of Fidelity

YOU'RE HOT, YOU say, from the drive, so you fill a glass with ice from the cooler and pull a bottle of Zinfandel from the paper sack by the bed. You do that Houdini trick with your bra—a few sighing, beneath-the-blouse contortions and you're free, pulling the thing from your sleeve. You down your drink, clink the ice around in the glass, and then you're in the shower.

When the cell phone rings, I know it's my wife. Before I pick it up. I can hear you talking to yourself in there above the noise of you coming clean—motel water slapping motel tile, words awash in the steam—so I close the bathroom door before I pick up.

Of course, she's crying. "You've been gone so long," she says.

"Honey," I say, "get hold of yourself. I only left at four."

I imagine that, back in Houston, she's sitting just where I left her, the oversized recliner in the den, her bathrobe bunched up high around her next-to-nothing hips.

"But where is everybody?" she says. "Where's Samantha?"

"I left her with Grandma," I say. "She's fine, honey. Did you take your pill?"

Then all I hear is the TV, the one she hasn't turned off in months. I go, "Honey?" but there's nothing but canned laughter from some sitcom. She's taken her meds, I think, and I'm wondering if maybe I should have hidden the bottle. The stuff makes her worse sometimes. She's like that—forgets she's had one and pops another. Sad, but I've seen her cry after downing enough Paxil to cheer up the whole of death row in Huntsville.

"You there?" I say, but it seems she's through with talking. I pull the phone away and look at the receiver. I think, Roaming charges, fifty cents a minute, and when I hang up there's that undertow of guilt I get in my guts, an ugly pull of regret at work beneath breaking waves of relief.

The water's off now, but you're still talking in there, asking questions, and in your voice is the kind of muffled uncertainty that always reminds me of hospital waiting rooms. Nights spent in lumpy vinyl chairs. A loved one gone from bad to worse. I lie back on the bed and stare at the cheap painting on the wall above the TV. There's this cowboy camped out somewhere on the prairie. The sun's going down, the horizon an eruption of western red, and he's stirring a pot over the campfire. Beans, I'm thinking. They always ate beans. What's strange, though: there's not even a horse. He's just sitting out there by his lonesome. Cooking. Waiting for nightfall. Not so much as an animal to keep him company.

"Baby?" you call from the bathroom. "Would you go for more ice? The cooler's about dry."

Outside, headlights flash and westbound rigs blast the motel with gusts of hot, diesel-laced air. A highway breeze. A woman laughs in the room next door. Through thin drapes, television blue washes onto the window and a man makes jokes in a pack-a-day voice, bringing up phlegm between one-liners. I stop to listen, but the window unit kicks on and drowns him out. I walk barefoot to the ice machine and press the bucket against the lever. The parking lot is almost empty. No one stops out here, halfway between Houston and Austin. I'm watching high clouds race each other east when ice starts falling over the rim of the bucket to my feet. I'm wondering why we drive seventy miles to spend the night together, why, when we're in the car, this little dive with its hand-painted Truckers Welcome sign and gravel drive is the earliest stop I can persuade myself to make.

Inside, you're wrapped in a towel on the bed. Two towels. You do that turban thing with one. You're asking, Did she call? Am I okay? I'm nodding and pouring wine and thinking of how my wife used to look after a bath. I'm remembering things you'd want to know—who she was, wet hair falling dark over flushed skin. White towels. The smiles of unwrapping. The faint birthmark high on the back of her thigh I used to kiss.

Later, you pull me onto the bed and feed me wine. We make hard, roadside love. You put your ear to my chest and listen to what's going on inside. Then you wait in the dark for me to say something, and when I don't, you whisper, "Penny for your thoughts."

I take a deep breath so you know I've heard. I touch your shoulder and shake my head and I think, No, they're still worth more than that.

Monuments

WHEN I WAS ten, after my mother left Dad and me and flew off to Europe, Kevin, the five-year-old next door, got run down in front of our house. He was chasing a cat, and after his body hit the pavement and slid into the grass near the Houston Lighting and Power substation across the road, neighbors say a bearded man in overalls stumbled down from the truck, put a hand on the sideview mirror to keep his balance, and took a leak right there in the street, beer cans falling from the cab to his feet. Later, we heard that Kevin's aorta had burst, that he probably hadn't felt the asphalt peeling his skin or the dark green cool of the grass where he'd come to a crumpled stop.

I didn't really know Kevin—he was so much younger than I was—but his sister and I were inseparable. Patty was the only kid in the fifth grade who could whip me at air hockey. She'd block my shots easily, humming along with the community center jukebox all the while, pressing her lips into a tight smile while she played, swirling her paddle in slow circles in front of her goal. Luring me off-guard with quick flicks of her tiny wrist, a teasing series of stops and false starts. Then she'd fire, launching a plastic streak of red into my goal so often that I accused her, under my breath, of cheating. Even now I can't honestly say if it was because her game impressed me, or because she sometimes let me cop a feel between her legs, but we acted in those days like conspirators, close and trusting, a little nervous nonetheless.

This was all in 1979, and Patty's long gone now. Just before junior high, when the bottom fell out of the Houston oil business, her father lost his job at Exxon and moved the family up north. Detroit, I think. After working my way through college, I landed a good job as an outside salesman, driving from one refinery to the next pitching high-dollar hose and couplings to men who wear tool belts and turn wrenches for a living, men like my father. Coming up fast on forty, I'm a long haul from childhood, but still the memories come. Sometimes when I'm on the road making sales calls, I'll find myself at the wheel of my truck, ten miles past my exit on the highway, nothing but steaming asphalt and thoughts of Patty in my wake, thoughts of the girl with sad black eyes and a tiny, upturned nose. The girl who loved me after Mom left.

• • •

Until that spring, Patty and I had been little more than neighbors, and though we walked together as we made our way to school or past the fire station to the community swimming pool, it was only because our mothers insisted. There was power in numbers, they said. Safety. And one, I'd heard Mom sing sometimes, was the loneliest number. "Besides," she said one morning before school, "little girls can't be walking around all by their lonesome like that. And I imagine you'd feel just awful if something happened to her, wouldn't you?"

That was it. Like it or not, Patty and I were bound by the buddy system.

Something changed, though, when Mom split. When Kevin died. Between our walk home from Deer Park Middle School and Dad's return from the afternoon shift at the refinery, Patty and I passed nearly all the twilight hours together in my room or out back in the yard, and in the damp morning we buddied up gladly on the sidewalk in front of her house before heading off to homeroom.

Of course, at school we acted like boys and girls do at that age, all spit and snarl on the outside, a swirl of curiosity churning away inside. But on the weekends, at night, Patty and I would move from the pallet of quilts Dad laid out on the floor up to my twin bed near the front windows. We pretended we were lost in a soft cave, flashlight beams whirling beneath the sheets. That, or we held each other and laughed, and sometimes, for a moment, with fingers slipped just inside the elastic of each other's pajama bottoms, we'd stop to ask permission with our eyes.

The first time it happened, Patty's breathing was so hushed and slow that I couldn't tell it from the seashell-sounding hum of trucks on the distant interstate. Our bodies tensed, alive with goose bumps despite the heat, charged with anxious electricity. Beneath my pajamas, Patty's fingers slid down past the swell of my stomach, wiggling playfully above where blood and heat were seized up and knotted together inside me. And then we turned face-to-face—our noses almost touching—and without blinking, without words, we listened to the merging confusion of sounds, to the traffic and heartbeats and the cool push of air conditioning from the overhead vents. Patty's pupils were dark, dilated, and when she looked down they sank like eclipsed moons to the low horizons of her eyes. Then we began, and Patty's fingers twitched, leaving a cool trail as they worked down and over me, tickling in such a wondrous and surprising and beneath-the-skin kind of way that the laughter never came.

Mostly, though, those nights in my room were spent talking about where we'd go when we were old enough to leave home. We stared out the window to the street and imagined places where there weren't refineries spilling smoke into the sky in such a way that it looked like they were feeding the clouds.

"I'm going to Looziana," I said one night. "Getting me a Trans-Am with an eagle on the hood. Going and eating gumbo like Aunt Norma makes. Gumbo every day."

"Been there," she said, pulling the miniblinds aside so that we could sandwich ourselves there between them and the windowpanes, pressing our noses to the steamed glass. "That's same as Texas, but with alligators and swamps."

"Where, then?" I said.

"Somewhere nice. Maybe Paris."

I imagined her sitting in a fancy restaurant, her skinny body stiff with false posture, speaking to another boy in a language I couldn't understand. All that blue water between us.

"That's where my mom's at," I said.

We ducked from beneath the blinds, and they slapped like hail against the window. Her eyes dropped to the sheets and she pulled a strand of black hair from her mouth.

She said, "Sorry," and she touched my leg. "I'm sorry."

That summer, near my eleventh birthday, we got word from Mom. One word. The morning she'd left, she called it a vacation. "Mama *needs* this," she'd said, dragging suitcase after suitcase down the front porch steps to the waiting taxi. "She deserves a vacation." Grandpa had died the year before, and I found out later she'd taken the money from his veterinary practice and gone off to cooking school. It was a dream of hers, and the night before she left, before Dad got home from work, she pushed her long red curls up into an enormous chef's hat she'd bought at the mall and pranced around the kitchen, smoothing a starched white apron down over her broad hips. "Tell me," she said. "Tell me, baby. Look at Mama. Don't you think she's too pretty to be stuck in this godawful town? To waste her cooking on a man who drowns his eggs in catsup?" It stung, the way she smiled when she said it, her mouth a sidelong oval of lipstick and satisfaction, like the words tasted sweet and red on her tongue. But even so, despite her smile and the tower of luggage blocking the hallway and the outbursts of ugliness I'd heard from my bed at night, I couldn't have imagined that she was going for good, that she was taking the kind of vacation mothers didn't come home from.

The day it came, Dad handed me a padded envelope he'd already opened. I remember feeling sorry for the ripped face of some woman on the stamps, remember feeling stupid for feeling sorry. Then I pulled out the card and a small ceramic replica of the Arc de Triomphe. Dad's eyes were on fire, burnt red and wet like he'd gotten a dose of the fertilizer mist while spraying the lawn.

"Keep it in your room," he said, his voice stern, pulled low by the weight of his anger, the same voice he used when he caught me playing with spray paint in the garage. "She sent it for you."

I remember carrying the thing tight against my chest and setting it on the trophy shelf in my room, tracing my thumb in the fine white network of decorative grooves and ridges. I don't remember, but I'm sure that in my excitement, and at my age, I didn't realize that the gift was also intended as a jab at my father. So many times I'd heard her tell him, the words drifting like heavy smoke under my door and into the bedroom night, "Don't think you're gonna keep me here, mister. Not now, you aren't. Should've gone years ago and that's a fact. Should've gone right off, pregnant and all."

The accompanying card was small, made from plain white paper, and the message inside was scrawled in pencil. It read, TRIUMPH!!! — just like that, three exclamation points — and I thought it was meant for me.

One evening late that summer, with the south Texas heat pressed down low by the chemical green sky, Patty and I were walking home from the community swimming pool with beach towels slung like heavy scarves around our necks, flip-flops snapping against our heels. We turned the corner onto our block and stopped to stare at a white cross that stood in the sod between the street and sidewalk in front of the light company. Loose soil was piled at its base so it seemed the thing had grown there in the heat of the afternoon, as if it had taken root and risen fast from the broken earth.

"What the hell?" I said, testing the feel of my father's words on my lips.

Patty's eyes were locked on the cross. She pulled the towel from around her neck and pushed it toward me as she started walking.

"It's a MADD cross," she said without turning back. "It's for Kevin."

To me, it didn't make sense. A mad cross? I thought, and all I could guess was that Patty's parents had done it, dug the hole and planted it there, some misplaced monument to their anger.

Patty stopped and turned to me, her dark eyes deep beneath tears, and she must have read the confusion on my face. "It's because he was drunk," she said. "They put them up all over. Mom says when you're drunk, it's never an accident."

As we stood before it, the cross looked bigger than it had from down the street. The top stood well above our waists. Crying, Patty reached down and touched her brother's name where it was etched into the bronze nameplate. She moved her fingers in the grooves while I stood shivering behind her, the wind licking sweat from my skin.

The only other time I saw Patty cry, we were playing our game in my bed, our bodies sandwiched between the windowpanes and the miniblinds. It was bright out, a big moon shining somewhere above our line of sight. I'd chosen California that night—I'd seen a surfing show on *Wide World of Sports*—but the car hadn't changed. I loved those Trans-Ams, that angry, flame-spitting bird.

"How about you?" I said.

She said, "There," and I had to ask *where* before I saw what she meant.

Her mother, who rarely left the house in those days, was struggling with a plastic bucket, holding on with both hands as she shimmied across the street, water and soap suds splashing her bare feet as she walked.

"What's she doing?" I said, but Patty touched my shoulder to shush me.

Setting the bucket in the grass, her mom lifted the hem

of her flowered summer dress up over her heavy calves and grimaced under her own weight as she knelt beside the cross. Her hair was silver with moonlight, cropped close but tangled by indifference and the shifting breeze. She sloshed her hands around in the water, wrung an over-sized sponge above the bucket, and began to wipe the cross with short, gentle strokes. Working her way to the base, she moved the sponge deliberately back into the bucket, wringing it slowly with both hands. Dabbing the white wood like you would a baby's cheeks after feeding.

Right then, with my lips on moonlit glass and my hand curved around Patty's waist, I imagined myself stiff and blue-lipped and dead underground, and my mother walking her barefoot way by, averting her eyes from my mud-caked stone and strolling past in a white windswept dress, the hem swirling around her freckled legs, her hair a blaze of sunlit red, her toes curling in the heap of new sod.

When Patty's mom finished, she struggled to her feet and smoothed the back of her dress with wet hands. She poured the remaining water around the base of the cross, and when she turned back toward the house we ducked from under the blinds. Patty was breathing like she'd just splashed up from under water, and I clicked on my flash-light to see tears sliding down the pale skin of her cheeks. My hands found hers in the tangled sheets, and she gripped me hard.

"She cleans his room, too," she said. "Every day. Dusts and mops and talks to him like he's sitting right there on the bed watching, and when I'm inside she gets onto me for not helping. Says I ought to lend a hand keeping things straight. Because he's too young, she says. Too young to do it himself."

This is what comes to me while I'm driving these Houston highways, what I imagine here in the haze of refinery smoke, what I hear beneath the hot hum of rubber rolling on asphalt. One moment I'm accelerating over the ship channel bridge, the next Patty's there in my room and I'm climbing from the bed, taking the little Arc de Triomphe from its shelf. And when I lay it in Patty's hands, she pulls it up against her chest.

"We'll go to Paris," I say, my palms against her cheeks. "We'll be fine." I don't believe it, but that's what I say, because it's the kind of hopeful untruth that means you're still breathing, still above ground, still alive enough to lie.

She nods, and we hold on to each other in a way that, looking back, seems a peculiar act for children. We stay like that, wrapped around each other, until the air conditioning snaps on in the attic and the sudden rush of air sweeps the last of our words from the room. Patty's hair smells clean—shampoo with a hint of apples—and I bring her in close so I can feel the dense beginnings of her breasts against my chest, and then I let go. With the moon out, the miniblinds carve us into slivers of light and shadow, and I feel the way it looks, like my body is ribboned with alternating bands of warmth and cold. And later, when her fingers slide beneath the waistband of my pajamas, my insides cinch tight, and I listen as she begins breathing in that quiet, familiar way. I work my hands down through the tangle of sheets and onto her skin. And when I lean forward, touching her nose with mine, I look up to find her eyes wide, two sad shadows, urging me on.

Among the Living Amidst the Trees

— For Lee K. Abbott

HALF PAST QUITTING time on Friday, a day we began by liquefying a family of possums in the debarker, and Garrett and me are driving the drive we drive five times a week. Route 96, from the paper mill in Silsbee, where we turn logs into loose-leaf, to Jasper, where we head home to shake the bark dust from our jeans and blow it from our noses and wash it from our hair before we take our women out for dancing and beer. Friday evening in the full steamy blaze of East Texas summer, and someone's gone and let those little lovebugs out from wherever it is they keep them holed up the rest of the year. Garrett's drinking a tallboy, working a toothpick around in his mouth and cursing the black mash of bug guts on his Silverado's windshield. He's scratching his wiry red sideburns like they're overrun with mites, glazing and smearing the front glass over again and again with the wiper-washers. "These sumbitches is freaks of nature," he says. "Fucking and flying what all at the same time."

"And dying," I say. Straight forward through the windshield I can't see a thing, not a bit of the road, but on either side the forest is wet and green and rustling with breeze. Garrett's leaning his head out the window now and then to get a better look at the road, cursing when he catches a bug in his teeth. I'm staring straight ahead into the aftermath of a bug orgy gone bad, and the whole time there's green streaking by in the corner of my eye — the trees, the undergrowth, a whole forest full of little live things waking up for the nightlife.

"Yessir," Garrett says. "Dying in mid-lay. Sounds good until you figure they probably don't even get their rocks off. They're probably just thinking those hold-on thoughts, you know, imagining about nuns or unpaid bills or a car crash, and then — Smack! Windshield. The great hereafter and beyond. All that shit."

"You think bugs even got rocks to get off?" I say.

Garrett takes his foot off the gas and shoots me a look like maybe I've slid over next to him on the bench seat and asked could I hold him awhile, then something outside catches his eye. "Well, whatever in blazing hell is wrong with the critters around here today?" he says, kicking hard on the brakes and sliding the truck to a stop on the gravel shoulder. "Possums all ground up like chili first thing in the morning. Fuck bugs. And now lookit," he says, tossing his empty back into the truck bed. "Lookit here at these dogs doing it human style."

And there they are, sure enough having canine relations right down in the ditch next to a rusty corrugated culvert, the one on top some sort of hound mix—part beagle, part blue tick, maybe—and so in need of a meal that from up on the highway he looks to be all rump and rib cage. His little bitch, she's missing an ear, and he's got her pinned down tight, her back against the far bank of the weed-choked ditch. The old boy, he's going at it in that churning-butter, dog-lay way. Even so, I can't help thinking there's a twinkle of something tender about these two, the way her front paws are wrapped up around the scruff of his collarless neck, the way he's intent on licking where her ear used to be all the while he has his way with her. And his way *is* a strange way, after all, for a dog. "They're doing it mission-ary," I say, and it seems silly to admit, but the whole thing slicks my guts with a kind of greasy, nervous guilt, the likes of which I haven't felt since my wife caught me playing my own fiddle in the shower one time last year. "Let's go," I say. "Give the old boy some privacy."

"Privacy?" Garrett says, fishing what's left of the six-pack from off the floorboards. "When you want privacy with Glenda, tell me something, you generally haul her out here to the side of the highway?"

Garrett's the kind of man who does more talking than thinking. Just this week, when one of these shirt-and-tie reporters who've come nosing around since the murder asked Garrett if he thought Jasper was a racist town, old Garrett looked into the camera and spit between his teeth. "Hell, no," he said. "We done elected blue-gums both as mayor and sheriff. Now what's that tell you?" Even so, Garrett every now and again makes good plain sense, so as crossways as it seems to be sitting on the side of the highway watching these dogs ravage one another, I've got to give the man his due. I crumple my empty and crack open a new can.

"Attaboy," says Garrett. "We ain't going nowhere. This is something you don't get to see but once, if ever, and we're gonna just sit right here and drink a cold beer and see it."

Afterward, on the way home, we decide we'd rather be drunk early than clean. We're halfway there as it is, and Conway Twitty's on the radio singing about whiskey and women and hasn't once yet mentioned a shower or soap, so there's maybe one of those subliminal messages working on account of that. Besides, the way all these reporters have been jammed into Slyder's Saloon since those sick bastards dragged Mr. Byrd down a rutted road until there wasn't anything left to drag, we figure we'd best get there early if we want a table level enough to set a longneck on. Instead of showering, once we clear the cloud of lovebugs, we crank down the windows to let the wind blast the dust from our hair. Outside, the sun is just beginning to hunker its way west, setting the treetops ablaze in such a way that the whole sky goes over to a kind of deep and waxy pink lipstick color. Garrett guns the engine and we speed toward home, breathing deep through our noses and shaking our befuddled heads at what we've just seen. It's a yeast farmer's wet dream out, too. The kind of hot and juicy you ought to be able to bottle and sell in drugstores. With the windows down, the forest smells akin to what you might get if you boiled Pine-Sol on the stovetop while roasting a sack of rain-soaked soil in the oven.

When we cross Route 190, Garrett veers left onto Main and spits out the window. Traffic's as heavy as it gets in a small town. High school kids with nowhere to be but on the streets, big sweating men trying to get home from work, all of it made worse by the news crews mulling around double-parked vans with their satellite antennas reaching up high as old pines, all of them just waiting for airtime so they can send word to the world of what a backward and bloodthirsty bunch of hicks we all are.

"If I was that dog," Garrett says, "I'd-a never let my lady know there was an alternative to the dog style. She's liable to get it in her head the old way's degrading or something, least if she's like Sandy she would. Hell, sometimes I get so tired of the same old thing I'd damn near do it on the side of the road just to spice things up, you know? Ten years of walking on that-time-of-the-month eggshells and what do I get? But you wouldn't know nothing about that, now would you, Mr. Newlywed. Your Glenda's a grinder, is she not?"

Now, maybe if someday we find ourselves making conversation somewhere in a locked-tight and soundproof and windowless room, and Garrett's tongue is tore clean out of his mouth and he's got both arms ground down to stumps so he can't write or do that sign language the deaf folks use, maybe then I'll tell him straight away that yes, he's absolutely right. A grinder, I'll say. No two ways about it. I'll tell him how matter-a-fact she *does* like to do it on the highway, preferably while I'm driving, and in the living room, with the lights on and the curtains thrown wide. In the ladies' room stall at Slyder's one Saturday night. I'll tell him about the rooftop, so help me God, when a new moon gave the night fully over to darkness and I arched myself beneath her, crawfishing my way backward, scooting up the shingled slope from eave to peak, all the while pressed between the hot sliding softness of my wife and the roof rash rising on my elbows and ass. I'll tell him about the shingle grit I'd picked grain by painful grain for a week from my skin.

Hell, put us in a room with no ears and I'll even embellish some things, but not now. Not here. In this little neck of the Big Thicket, words bounce around from tree to tree, house to house, and mouth to blathering mouth, so I don't say a thing. A year back, the night before Glenda and I got married, her daddy, Tricky, threw us a party at Slyder's, rented the whole place out. This was in the days before he found out about his cancer, before his black hair turned loose of its gray scalp, and when he pulled me a new Lone Star from the ice and twisted her open, he put his big, thick-skinned hand on the back of my neck and told me to be careful where I let my mind wander, especially when Glenda wasn't around to keep it penned up. Glenda's mom, he told me, had run out on him because he one time *thought* about cheating. He said news — true or otherwise — travels that damn fast or faster here in Jasper. Said all he was doing was having a dirty daydream about the new drive-thru girl at the Cream Burger, and when he got home the old lady had cleared out. "And all I done," Tricky said, holding his beer bottle like a microphone, "was lean in a little when this gal handed me my lunch so I could see what she had working under her shirt."

That's just the way it is around here, so I don't tell Garrett a thing. I don't mention how in the early days, after I'd run into Glenda at the Easy Clean Laundromat she inherited from her grandma and we'd been out a time or two, she took to taunting me. About how one night, while we walked along Coon Creek out back of my place, she'd crouched behind a sweet gum tree and stepped out of her dress before wading through the tangle of shoreline shadows and into the water. "Come on," she said, working water with cupped hands over her moonlit skin. "Get in here. You aim to be a man tonight or not?"

Instead, I let Garrett drive and I drink what's left of my beer and I try not to think too much about Glenda, about how her skin shines even in the darkness, even beneath the water; about how Garrett's wife, Sandy, spends her lunch break away from the police station filing room where she works and eats instead at the laundromat, where she fills my wife's head with the latest horror stories about the way

James Byrd was killed, about the root-riddled road that ripped his body apart as he thrashed and slid, chained behind his murderers' truck; about how Mr. Byrd used to smile and whistle while washing his work clothes on Sunday nights; about how Glenda's started talking lately about going out to Huff Creek Road so she can see where it happened, so she can smother her imagination in the reality of it, no matter how gruesome; about how tore up she gets nights on account of her daddy and his cancer; about how some nights she lets loose to crying even while we're making love, and how it hollows me out so that I think nothing will ever fill me up again.

Some nights I'll sleep in restless fits, the muscles of my lower back burning with spasms so that I dream I'm an animal with a boot on my neck and a red iron searing another man's initials into my hide. Every night this week, after I think she's cried herself to sleep, I've jerked awake to a bed half full and the sound of her voice in the hall. Even over the telephone, Tricky will have her in stitches, and through the cool hum of the air conditioner her quiet laughter will push its way into the room. I'll prop myself up in bed and feel the kinks in my back turn loose. And I'll listen, trying to imagine what he's saying, how he's managing to make her laugh.

"I can't push it out of my mind," Glenda will tell him. "I'm serious, Daddy. I keep seeing it. Over and over. His body tearing apart on that road, and it's not like I knew him that well, but I keep expecting him to walk into the store and set his laundry bag on one of the machines and nod and smile at me while he feeds dollars into the change machine. I keep hearing his whistling. He had such a pretty way of whistling, so high and sweet for a man his size, and he wasn't showy about it, either. You could tell he wasn't doing it for anyone but himself."

And then she'll stop talking and start listening, her bare feet sliding across the hardwoods while she paces, her breathing loud enough to hear, and then she'll let loose the slightest of half-swallowed laughs. "It's just that I don't know what I'm ever going to do without you," she'll say, and I'll wonder how a man gets to be man enough to hear that and go on telling jokes. Man enough to give of himself exactly what's needed.

You aim to be a man tonight or not? It stings more than a little to think about it, but as Garrett pulls into the back lot behind Slyder's and tilts the rearview down so he can watch himself run a comb through his tangle of red curls, all I can think is that more and more, when I'm alone with my wife, it's not the wild sex I'm after. I don't want all the gymnastics or the risk of being seen or the shingle grit stuck in my skin. Instead I want her to laugh, to wink at me while stepping out of her skirt, to turn off the lights and shut the bedroom door and pull me with her beneath three or four quilts so that I can have her all to myself, so I can duck my head beneath the covers before we make love and see her skin glowing there in the darkness, calling to me in some shiny new language only I can understand, lighting my way while I reach out and hold her and keep her from crying and answer her in the voice of the man I've somehow managed to become.

Inside, standing back of the bar, Stu Slyder is damn near salivating at all the business coming his way on account of this murder. If you'd lived here all your life like I have, and you happened upon Slyder's tonight, aiming to have a long sit-down with the boys over a few cold ones, you'd no doubt stop at the door and marvel awhile, wondering if you'd taken a wrong turn somewhere, maybe stumbled across some secret white-collar society in your yellow-dog town. There are guys in neckties everywhere. Back at the pool table. Bellied up to the bar. And instead of the familiar stink—sawdust and sweat and spilled tap beer—the place is ripe with the smell of aftershave. Stu is smiling his gap-toothed smile, trying to keep his shirt tucked in despite the downward slump of his belly. He's sliding bottles across the bar, slicking the stray hairs of his comb-over back with the palm of his hand. It don't take much of a man, I'm thinking, to get rich off his hometown's troubles.

Garrett makes his way back from the bar and hands me a longneck. "Lookit that leech," he says. "Teeth on him, he could eat corn on the cob through a picket fence, and *would* too if he thought he could make a buck doing it. Promise him ten dollars for the pleasure and he'd kiss your ass on the steps of city hall and give you an hour to draw a crowd."

"He counts all his money after tonight," I say, "the price is liable to go up."

"Sounds about right," he says. "He's a counter, sure enough. Always did like that math. Sucked up to Mrs. Earlich so bad in algebra class you'd have thought her big tits reached out all the way to his desk."

Looks of Stu's new brick house up on the highway, I'm thinking, maybe we all should have sucked a little of that tit. He's a tight-ass, all right, but he ain't stupid. Besides, this is the only bar in town with a dance floor. And they still got Bob Wills on the jukebox. And then there's Glenda's daddy, Tricky, huddled as per usual around the big corner table with his fellow pipe fitters playing forty-two, every one of their heads sheared clean as summertime sheep. They're slapping dominoes on the tabletop and scratching the backs of their necks and no doubt comparing notes on the Harleys they've got ready to roll out back. Six months back, after Tricky's first couple chemo sessions, all the boys of the pipe fitters' local shaved their heads. It was a hard man's brand of brotherhood, and the night they did it Tricky walked into the bar, and when he saw them his eyes filled with a liquid look of something like love. These are rough-hewn and heavy men, men with calluses thick as rawhide, men who aren't afraid to keep something tender beneath their rib cages, and to expose it to the elements when occasion calls for it, no matter how it hurts. Tonight, it's these men and their laughter and the cold bite of beer on my teeth that set me at ease, despite the fact that Stu Slyder is talking quiet-like to one of these hair-gelled reporters, leaning in close enough to kiss the guy. He reaches across the bar and takes a sharply creased greenback from the man, some high denomination, I'm guessing, and I catch Garrett's eye and nod in that direction.

"A value-added whore," Garrett says. "I shit you not. Put a quarter in his ear and his teeth fold back."

"Save us some seats over by Tricky," I say. "I'll call the girls."

Garrett nods and I make my way to the pay phone in the back near the ladies' room. As soon as Glenda picks up the phone she says, "Where are you and why aren't you here?"

"Got sidetracked," I say. "We hit some gravel on the way home, started sliding and slid clean over to Slyder's. Go get Sandy and meet us here, would you?"

"Figured as much," she says. "Already got the quilt in the truck, so don't get too drunk on me. I got plans for you yet tonight."

"Looks of this place," I tell her, "the whole world's got plans tonight, and they mostly include Slyder's. You wouldn't believe the out-of-towners."

"Well, hang in there, old-timer. I'm on my way. Is Daddy there?"

"Him and the whole crew."

"Well, then it can't be *that* bad. They'd just as soon drink water as mingle with strangers."

"Then keep your headlights on bright when you pass over Coon Creek and you oughta see them all bending down for a drink. I'm serious, sugar. I ain't ever seen the likes of this. I keep thinking of what my cousin Ty said after that school bus went into the ravine last year out his way and all those kids drowned. He likened living in Harlingen that week to being in the freaking zoo, and on the wrong side of the bars, too. Strangers gawking at you, getting on the TV and twisting things all around."

"Now hold on, baby doll," Glenda says. "I'm coming. If something's going to get twisted tonight, it better be me around you."

Back at the table, Garrett's holding forth with Tricky and the boys, throwing his hands around like he's on a Sunday-morning church show and something holy's taken hold of him. I grab a couple new beers from the bar, and when I sit down he winks at me, popping a toothpick into his mouth. Next to Tricky are the Hooper twins, DJ and Teke, and their cousin Nelson, three massive men with shining scalps. You put this foursome in the bed of a pickup, the bumper would throw sparks going down the road. Now Garrett works his toothpick around in his molars awhile, then he plucks it from his mouth and points it at me. "So then the foreman, old Henderson, he tells us to fire up the debarking drum, and it ain't but seven-thirty and already it's hot as the devil's dick out, and let me tell you something about your son-in-law here, Tricky. He reckons he'll stand right in front of the debarker's vents while I run the first load of logs, figures he'll get a blast of fresh sappy air in his hair when I hit the pneumatics. So I crank that big bastard up and load it with pine and tumble them logs barkless and clean, real quick work, but when I release the valves and the vents spring open, all I hear is this poor boy cussing and carrying on. I mean, he's howling, so I shut

the machine down and haul ass around to him thinking
something's gone wrong, maybe he's hurt, and there he is,
bloody as a blind butcher. Shit's in his eyes. He's spitting
it out his mouth. And then it hits me. It's them possums
again. We've caught them nesting time to time in the debarker drum when the heat gets bad. And I shit you not, we
must've tore a half dozen or more of them little sumbitches
to shreds."

Garrett stops now for effect while the boys start chuck-
ling, looking at me sidelong, then he tilts his beer back and
slams it empty on the table. Even I can't help but smile.
"Yessir," he says. "Tricky, your boy here was wearing pos-
sum insides *all over* his outsides."

It's when the women show up that things begin to get ugly,
but not on account of them. Sandy, she's decked out with
that black hair pulled back tight as the skirt that's riding
up on those wide, hand-hold hips. Garrett talks a lot of
lonesome-man trash, but his woman's got on her the kind
of grade-school-teacher good looks that can drive a man
to mischief when he's alone in the shower. As for Glenda,
her hair's done up in pigtails. Her skin, it's got the sheen
of something well-buttered to it, something so shining and
bright you could kill the main to Slyder's breaker box out
back, and so long as she was there, you'd still have enough
light to drink by. They're lovely, the both of them, and they
don't mind hearing it.

"There's my girl," Tricky says, pushing himself back

from the table and slapping a palm against his knee. "Ain't she a peach?"

Glenda smiles, puts a hand on her hip and bats her eyes, then plops into his lap. "I'll bet you say that to all the girls who get your laundry done free for you."

"Sure do," he says, playing a domino from his hand. "Thing is, unless something's changed around here, and things rarely do, every girl who fits that bill has got her ass right this minute in my lap."

"How you feeling, Daddy? You know you're not supposed to be drinking a bunch of beer."

"Well it ain't going to kill me, now is it?" he says.

DJ and Teke raise eyebrows at each other and reach for their cigarettes. Nelson smoothes a hand over his shaved scalp, says, "You're too damn stubborn to die, you old fart, so quit talking your sympathy talk and shake the dominoes. These women came to dance, no doubt, not to hear your bellyaching."

DJ and Teke nod and blow smoke from their noses. Garrett and me, we take the hint and haul our ladies to the dance floor, or what's left of it, given the crowd. Somebody's gone and paid a half dollar to hear Willie Nelson sing about blue eyes and rain showers and heartbreak, and when Glenda leans her head back into the crook of my elbow I can smell the honeysuckle lotion she smoothes into her skin after showering. She tickles her fingers on the back of my neck while we turn and slide around the floor. On her face, wet-eyed worry.

"That Willie Nelson knows a thing or two," she says, closing her eyes.

"So do you," I whisper.

Six months back, when Tricky came straight from the doctor's on a Saturday afternoon to give us the bad news, Glenda and I were making love in the shower, and while we dance and Willie sings and Glenda leans forward, pressing her face to my chest, I'm in two places at once. My feet are sliding in time to the music, but my mind is under that spray of water with her, both of us lathered with soap, Glenda with a foot up on each side of the tub so she could bend her knees and lower herself down onto me while I blinked water from my eyes and held her hips, watching them fall and rise. "Every time we come here it's raining," she'd said, working herself against me. It's an old joke between us, one that deserved its silly little answer. "Every time it rains here we're coming," I told her. Then the door rattled and the muscles in Glenda's hips twitched and Tricky's voice was hot and thick as the bathroom steam. "You rabbits get on out of there," he said. "I've got something needs telling."

And now, as Willie winds it down and Garrett and Sandy dance over close to bump hips with us and laugh, Glenda lifts her face back from my chest and I see her dark eyes are drowning, and still she manages a smile. "I was thinking about your daddy catching us in the shower," I tell her.

She takes my hand and we stand there awhile, waiting for the next record to play. "I was thinking about Mr. Byrd," she says. "Sandy says they had to hunt with dogs for the missing pieces. Spent half a day drawing spray-paint circles on the ground where they found his dentures or keys, a hand with a ring still on its finger—like that. Can you imagine?"

"I can't," I say, sliding her into the first three steps of a waltz. I mean to say something else, but instead a hard little fist of muscles starts clinching down low in my back, and I'm listening to the whisk of our boots on the dance floor and holding my wife a little too tight for good dancing, and all I can think about is those dogs on the side of the highway, about how the one on top took the trouble to lick clean his little woman's wound, about how even animals find ways to be kind.

I loosen my grip on Glenda's hand and lead her into a spin. Her pigtails whip the air and the hem of her dress parachutes out and she lets loose of a little squeal. I reel her back in, stepping long on the hard note of the waltz as I pull her in tight. She slips her fingers into the back pocket of my jeans, and I'm about to tell her about the dogs, about how Garrett called their position human style, but that's when the music stops, and so do we.

We stop and turn and Stu Slyder is standing by the juke-box with the electrical cord in his hands. He's turning up the television set over the bar with the remote control. Up there on the screen is the slick-haired man I saw earlier pressing creased money into Stu's hand, and he's standing now in front of Slyder's, his lips curled up in such a way that folks in living rooms all over God's creation will know that it pains him just to be here, to be standing amidst our kind. This whole town stinks something fierce, he might as well be saying.

"Turn that mess off," Garrett hollers, but Stu's not having any of it.

"Fixing to be *Candid Camera*," he says, "so y'all be on your best behavior."

On the television, the reporter is gesturing wildly, talking about the town and the men who'd spent many of their adult years in prison. "For all we know, the murder could have been planned in this very bar," he tells us. "This is where the suspects were arrested. Just out back of where I stand right now, in the parking lot, police tell us that the blood-spattered chain they allegedly used to drag the victim to his death was recovered from the bed of the suspects' truck."

Glenda steps close behind me, reaching her arms around my waist. Stu Slyder is taking baby steps toward the television set, beaming at this windfall of publicity. The bar, loud and alive with talk and music a minute ago, is now taken with the kind of quiet you mostly hear in churches or hospitals.

"Channel Three News has since learned that the blood found on the chain and on one of the suspect's shoes matches the type of the victim, James Byrd Jr., and we have reports that other members of the upstart Aryan group have been known to frequent this establishment."

"What a bunch of horse shit," Garrett says.

Then the reporter opens the door and we begin to see

ourselves on the television screen. I stand there stunned, my toes gone numb in my boots while the camera pans around the room and there I am, wide eyes rimmed in red, my work shirt faded and frayed near the embroidered nametag. Glenda's visible only as arms wrapped around my waist, and then we're gone, off screen, just like that, and I see what the reporter wants the world to see, a table full of hulking, hard-looking men with shaved heads and lit cigarettes, dominoes standing in rows before them. Tricky and Nelson and the Hooper twins, they sit there fixed in the lights of the camera while this reporter talks about the Aryan Nation and the KKK and skinheads, and when Glenda pushes me out of her way and stomps over to the camera, for a moment I watch her, the real her, and then I turn back to the television and see her there, her pigtails bobbing behind her as she spits at the reporter and swings around to point a finger at the cameraman, and at me — at all of us glued to the screen.

"They ain't skinheads, you asshole!" she screams. I'm right there, not ten feet from her, but what I feel instead of pride or love or some impulse to protect her is an acid-hot drip in my guts, a kind of embarrassment you feel for people you don't know when they come unglued on afternoon talk shows. "That's my daddy," Glenda says, and then she's flailing away at the camera and Tricky is up in a hurry, wrapping her in his big sunburned arms, and I just stand there, the only one left watching the screen, marveling at the television version of my life.

It's not until Stu Slyder steps in that I snap out of it. He's up there onscreen, his fat blue tongue visible through the gap in his teeth as he moves between the camera crew and Glenda, as he stutters and sputters and rants about the First Amendment and then—never mind that Tricky's got her in his arms, never mind that it's all under control—then the fat bastard leans in with two rigid fingers and thumps Glenda up high on the chest, just below the tender skin of her neck, and that's all it takes.

I haven't hit anyone since high school, haven't been hit since my father one time backhanded me in the jaw for getting smart with him about something I can't even remember anymore. But tonight it comes so natural I would swear it's something you're born with, the backward snap of the elbow, the instinctive grip of the other man's collar. The spill of adrenaline into your veins when you make blood spray from another man's nose. My knuckles crack with the impact, and the sound of it is sharp as the fireside pop of hickory kindling, only louder. His head, it snaps back and I jump him, slamming him to the floor. He's on his back, pinned down with that ridiculous flap of comb-over hair dangling around his ear, and I keep throwing punches, knocking his big head against the hardwoods with each blow until his eyes glaze over with a bloodshot brand of fear I've never seen before.

Then he kicks his legs hard and throws all his weight to one side and I'm caught for a moment off-balance, reaching down to catch myself when he throws himself forward, slamming his forehead into my mouth, and I don't know if the cameras are still rolling or not, don't know if Glenda is burrowing her face into Tricky's chest or staring down at me with the same kind of unease I'd felt for her not a minute before. All I know is that my eyes are awash with hot white light, and that I've got blood in my mouth for the second time in a single day, and that mine tastes sharply of iron, and that Garrett is leaning down and hoisting me up by my belt, saying, *Holy shit, hoss, that was a serious big can of whup-ass,* and that when my vision comes back the first thing I see is the reporter with his microphone at his side and his eyes on the floor, probably praying I'm done swinging for the night.

Then we're making a break for it, shuffling past the pay phone for the back door, getting the hell out of there. In the parking lot, the moon is throwing light off the chrome of the pipe fitters' Harleys as they kick them to life. Garrett's laughing hard, howling into the night, asking, *When did you get to be such a shit kicker?* as he loads Sandy into his truck and cranks it up. Glenda shoots me a long and blinking and altogether confused look, a look you might give your husband if, say, you caught him jerking off in the shower, then she climbs up into the driver's seat of my truck and slams the door. I circle around to the passenger side, breathing in the exhaust of all these loud engines, and before I get in I spit a fat wad of blood into the parking lot gravel, and there, at my feet, half a tooth floats yellow and broken in a thick pool of red.

In the truck, I don't know what to expect. A stern talking-to, maybe. A ride home and a night spent alone in bed while

Glenda walks the halls talking quietly into the telephone. Instead, there's an unexpectedly cool swirl of air pouring in through the windows and, outside, a drift of clouds running up on the moon. There's the hum of tires on concrete and the rumble of the engine through residential back roads to the outskirts of town, where Glenda steers over an old logging bridge and puts the headlights on bright and slows to a crawl, centering the truck on the dirt road while we bounce in and out of ruts and over roots and the chassis squeaks and shimmies. "Not afraid of ghosts," Glenda says, "are you, sugar?"

I inhale and the night air saws away at the exposed nerves of my tooth. Tree branches lean in to brush the truck's front quarter panels. Glenda, she keeps on driving.

"Don't know," I say. "Never met one."

A mile or so up, the road is roped off with yellow police tape. Glenda kills the engine and grabs the flashlight from beneath the seat. "Night like tonight," she says, "can't get any weirder, I'm thinking."

I climb down from the truck and duck under the tape, following my wife as she pans the flashlight beam from one side of the road to the other. All around us there's the clatter of falling branches and the hissing of the breeze and the frogs speaking up from the trees. The road falls off on each side into ditches littered with weeds and debris, and I begin to wonder just how the hell you can drive a man into these woods and drag him from your truck, how you can cave his head in with the heel of your boot and then hold him down, your knee on the back of his neck, while your buddies hitch chains to his ankles. I'm wondering how you can stand over him—no matter what damn color he is, no matter what you believe—smoking a cigarette until he comes to and you see the fear widening in his eyes. I'm trying to imagine how it might have played out, how it all might have looked, but what I see instead are Stu Slyder's bloodshot eyes, and now I'm wondering just what the hell I'd been thinking back at the bar.

Up ahead, Glenda stops and squats over a red ring painted onto the hard-cooked dirt. "Dear God," she says, shining the light up the road. "Look at them all."

And there, by God, they are: dozens of them, some big enough to outline a trash can lid, others so small you could cover them with a coffee cup, and no pattern or order to them whatsoever. We walk up the road and Glenda bounces the light around from red circle to red circle, and the moon stays back behind the clouds, and the forest seems rightfully alive and loud. And they just go on forever. I'm thinking you could pull me apart however you pleased, and no matter how you tried you'd never end up with enough pieces to fill these rings. I'm thinking there's a lesson in that, a lesson I might could stand to learn, something about how there's always more to you than what you might think, but then Glenda bends down and traces a finger around one of the red circles and it's all I can do to stand there and watch her.

"He could whistle like you wouldn't believe," she says, "a not-a-care-in-the-world kind of whistle, the same way Daddy used to." She looks back at me with an arm outstretched, and when I go to her there's nothing left but to get down on my knees there beside her in the dirt and watch while she flattens out her hand and rubs this circle of paint into the earth. "Just whistling like that," she says, wiping her hand on my jeans, "ought to be enough to keep you alive."

On the walk back, Glenda turns the flashlight off. I freeze and look around long enough to see that I can't see a thing, so I bring her in tight, and I hold her there in the darkness, and when she leans her head back from me I get ready to walk. But then her lips are on me, and they're open, and my mouth is all of a sudden so full of her that it's like I'm being kissed all at once by everyone in my life who ever loved me in the least.

Back at the truck, Glenda throws a quilt down in the bed and we undress each other there in the dark before climbing in. It's habit, something I'm so accustomed to that I don't question it until we're wrapped up together with the quilt over our heads, until she pulls one of my legs up between her own and I can feel her there, the soft and swollen wetness of her. Her breath pushes hot against my chest and my tooth is screaming, a sharp pain that burrows down through the meat of my gums and into my jaw, and I want like hell here to tell Glenda that we don't have to do this, that we can just lie here awhile and go to the house, that I understand what just happened out on this road. Truth is, though, that I can't put it into words, not just yet, and all I know is that her skin is so soft it pains me to even think about letting her go, and her breathing is steady and slow, the breath of the deeply dreaming, and I'm thinking she might sleep through the night for the first time all week. Still I can sense that she's waiting, waiting for me to say something, so I tell her the first thing that comes to my muddied mind. "Garrett and me," I tell her. "We saw a couple dogs today. Up on Route 96. Doing it missionary."

She rolls back, pulling me up onto her. She presses her mouth against my cheek and I can feel her smiling there in the dark. She whispers, "You did not," and slips me inside.

I close my eyes, swallowing hard as I push myself into her. "Did too," I say, and then we're wrapped up in warmth, wrapped up in each other and in the sounds of the forest around us, the wind and the trees and the insects almost mechanically loud, like they've been working all night to find the right riff, and with a little work I hear them not as a whole but as single instruments, the same way you can when you focus in to find the bass line as you step onto the dance floor, so your feet know whether to polka or two-step or waltz. Except something's not right. Here I am, a man making slow love to his wife in the back of a pickup truck not half a mile from where another man was just this week murdered, and the forest has something too deep to its melody, something too low-down and rumbling. Despite the quilt over our heads, it's all of a sudden a slightly brighter night, and I'm sure, right up until the voice bounces around in the trees, that the moon's found its way out of the clouds.

But then it comes, my name called out like it's a question

all in itself, and for the second time tonight I'm thinking
about how Tricky caught us in the shower, only this time
I'm not remembering it so fondly. This time I'm feeling
again the hot flush of my ears and the nervous twitching
in Glenda's hips, the way time stops for just a sliver of a
second when two grown people who love each other freeze
in the middle of their most private moment and hope like
hell they're both hearing things. It's settling into me the
way grit can settle into a man's skin that headlights don't
feel the same as moonlight, and then I hear it again.

"Hey, bud," Garrett says. "You in there?"

I duck out from the covers, throwing the quilt over
Glenda, and when she pokes her head out her pigtails are
frazzled with static. She looks like a schoolgirl who's been
caught by her daddy doing back-seat, midnight things, and
I feel something warm and altogether newly formed bal-
looning wide in my chest. "Nice timing," I say, and Garrett comes over, his truck's headlights throwing his long
shadow over us as he walks our way scratching a toothpick
around in his sideburns.

"Hell, you two," he says, "ain't enough *ever* enough?"

Glenda smiles without showing teeth, and I can tell she's
not embarrassed. I can tell she's flattered, flattered to be
young and wild and lovely enough yet to make even the
likes of Garrett shake his head with envy.

Now the moon really does come skulking out from the
clouds, and when my tooth throbs I realize I'm smiling.
Glenda's toes are curling around in my leg hairs, telling a
little joke of their own, and when I look over, her lips are

pressed into a girlish grin and it's clear that she's more than happy to let me do the talking.

When I look back at Garrett he's shuffling his boots in the dirt. His eyes shift quick from Glenda to the ground.

"Out looking for more dogs to gawk at?" I ask.

"I wish," he says.

"What, then? They looking for me back in town?"

"They are," he says, and then he turns to Glenda. "They already came by our place. Sandy said you had some wild idea about coming out here and having a look."

"She's got lots of wild ideas," I tell him, but Garrett just rolls his eyes and keeps talking. Old Stu's hot, he's saying, wanting to press charges, wanting some payback. "I dropped Sandy at the police station on the way. She thinks maybe she can talk Sheriff Duecker into cutting you some slack, but all the same I wanted to warn you. You'd be in a fast river of shit if they found you out here."

"They bothered Tricky and them yet?"

"I doubt it. They tore off toward the highway when we ditched the bar. They're probably bellied up to another game of forty-two down in Kirbyville by now."

"Well, hell," I tell him, standing up in the bed of the truck. "I better get on into town then and turn myself in before they get back. Last thing Tricky needs is to come home to cops at his door and people talking all over town about his son-in-law the fugitive."

Glenda leans back against the cab and shakes her head. Her eyes water and sparkle in such a way that I know she's trying hard not to laugh. "I don't guess they'll need to frisk you," she says, and I look down at myself, a man with flecks of sawdust in his chest hair, a man wearing nothing but moonlight and pale skin and not-so-white socks. A man I don't yet fully recognize.

"I hate to do it, Glenda," Garrett says, "but I'm going to turn my back now so you can get dressed." And then he does. He turns and walks away and waits with his back turned, leaning on the door of his truck while Glenda fishes around in the quilts and hands me my jeans. I stand there awhile before putting them on, and I wink at my wife, and I look out into the forest where the crickets and frogs are still carrying on.

"You gonna bail me out?" I ask, and Glenda grins as I step into my pants. She stands, letting the quilt fall away from her. "I believe I will," she says, and I nod and smile and buckle my belt, and her skin is shining so bright and warm it's a wonder I don't melt.

What You're Walking Around Without

— FOR MELANIE RAE

I F IN THE last ten years you've lived within a hundred miles of Houston along the southwest corridor of Highway 59, and in that time you've had a breast removed, or both, or you've had a hysterectomy or a lumpectomy or a swollen purple mole dug from your skin, then this is true: Whatever your surgeon cut out of you spent some time with Dean Covin in his car.

They put the breasts in quart-sized plastic containers with snap-on lids, the kind of cheap Tupperware Dean hopes they don't reuse. A uterus warrants a half-gallon bucket. Ovaries and tumors bob and float in pint-sized containers filled with gray liquid preservative. On a busy day—say, a Friday, like today—between his two insulated totes, Dean will have bits and pieces of forty people sloshing around on the back seat by the time he makes it from

Victoria to Deer Park, where he rolls slow into the neighborhood, pulling into the driveway of the house his injuries have purchased for him.

Once parked, he cracks the window so he'll be able to hear the dispatcher, Luanne, bantering with the other drivers on the radio. He leaves the engine running, the totes on the seat, the a/c blasting to keep the car cool while he grabs a can of beans from the pantry and sits spooning them into his mouth on the front porch. Today, as always in August, the sun is blazing, and Dean's ears are humming with the overhead heat. He sweats and blinks and thinks back to the day he slipped on a ladder and tumbled fifteen feet to the floor of a Gulf Coast drilling rig's void tanks, to the moment he awoke in the spotlight of sun that came with God through the portal above, to the hum in his ears and the twitching in his extremities. Now he watches these loud and lanky neighborhood kids, children enjoying their summer break from school, jumping bicycles over a makeshift ramp in the street, sliding on plastic garbage bags over sprinkler-slicked lawns of St. Augustine.

If you live on this street, if your husband is working the day shift at the Exxon or Phillips plant across the highway, if you keep the television volume muted so you can hear if the evacuation sirens start screaming, then you've told your kids to steer clear of Dean Covin. There's something not right about him. Wears that brace on his wrist to squeeze off the shakes. When he's mowing his lawn, that eye, the one that rolls untethered in its socket, seems always to follow you from carport to porch when you carry your groceries inside. And his face, it jolts sometimes with a tic, like he's got electricity pulsing through him for no reason at all. Leave him be, you've said. Ain't a reason on earth for you to pester a man like that.

For the most part the children listen, but there's always one.

Dean Covin stands, drops the plastic spoon into the empty can, drops the can into the garbage by the garage, and gets back in his car, a two-year-old Chrysler with six-digit mileage from his daily route, a blue car with enough clear-coat shine to trigger suspecting looks in this pickup-truck neighborhood. But what's it matter? Dean thinks. The car's got enough room up front so he can hit the cruise control and stretch his bad leg on the longer straightaways of 59. That alone's worth a crossways look or two. He checks in on the radio, lets Luanne know he's back on the road. "Ninety-six," he says.

"Ninety-six, go ahead."

"I'm ten-seven from the house, Luanne. Should make the lab in half an hour."

"Ten-four, Ninety-six. Try not to get lost."

That Luanne, Dean thinks. Now there's a woman. Black hot-dipped jeans and a red-lipped smile. Sense of humor, too. Oh, what he wouldn't give. He turns the radio down and checks the rearview. Behind him, a kid he knows gets up to speed on his bike, aims it at the ramp in the street, then bails off at the last minute, rolling on the concrete and hopping to his feet as the bike launches itself aloft un-manned before it crashes and slides, spitting sparks, on its side. The other kids stand silently street-side, as if Jesus himself has descended to perform a BMX miracle. A tiny, scraped-kneed girl with red pigtails makes a break for her porch across the street and disappears inside.

This boy, John Dalton, pumps his fist in the air. "Shit, yeah!" he screams. "Nice." Then he spits in the street, leaves his bike in a heap, and struts up the drive toward Dean Covin's car, working a plug of bubblegum around in his mouth the way a big league pitcher might. This kid walks bowlegged, wears an old orange Astros cap backward on his burr-cut head. He spits a good deal, Dean's noticed, like at eleven years old he's already tasted something he can't quite wash clean from his mouth. Yes, he's a sour little guy, sneering and squinting all the time. Still, he's the only one on the block who will return so much as a look from Dean, and as the boy sidles up to the car Dean rolls his window down and the hum in his ears begins to recede, pulling itself back into him until it's barely distinguishable from the idling engine.

"What you got in the coolers today?" John Dalton says, leaning into the car. "Anything nasty?"

Two weeks before, Dean Covin had peeled one of the plastic container lids back and let the boy poke a floating breast with the eraser end of his pencil. "Bet you haven't seen the likes of this," he'd said.

The boy had smiled with only the chapped corners of his lips, pushing the tissue down into the liquid, widening his eyes a bit when it came bobbing, buoyant, back to the surface. "Have too," John Dalton said. "All the time."

Now, every day, the boy wants more. Dean prays about it, frets about it in bed, but the boy is only curious, a kind of curious Dean understands, and though he steels himself against it the same way he promises himself he'll quit smoking—*tomorrow, so help me God*—he can't tell this boy no.

Dean turns up the country and western station on the radio. Loud, but not so loud that he can't hear Luanne on the two-way. He pushes in the lighter and reaches into the back seat, fishing around in one of the totes. "What do you want?" he asks.

John Dalton sucks snot back into his throat and spits on the driveway. "An eyeball," he says. "A big slimy one."

Dean laughs, lights his cigarette, pulls a container from the tote and tries to steady it with his good hand so it doesn't slosh around. "We don't do eyes," he says. "They keep them alive. Give them to people who need them. Blind people, so they can see."

"Yeah, right," the boy says. "Whatever. Another boob then, I guess."

Dean pops the lid, says, "I thought so," and hands John Dalton the pencil.

After his specimen drop at the lab, after Dean Covin calls Luanne to let her know he's ten-eight and available for local STAT runs, while he waits, drumming his fingers on the steering wheel and listening to the two-way for his next job, he slides the pencil from behind his ear, double-checks his specimen log for the day. He pulls his spiral notebook from beneath the seat and transcribes the list of names. Most are women, most are always women, as if their bodies more often betray them, or are, as Dean sometimes thinks, more generous, more giving of themselves, as if these women look up from their gurneys, the anesthesia sliding cold through the IV line, and what they find bubbling up from the glazed-water surfaces of their minds is something that makes them wet their lips and, out of selflessness or some unnamable desire, whisper to the surgeon, *Please, just take what you need.* Dean runs the fingers of his good hand over the new list of names. It has been twelve years since he touched a woman—a real woman, a whole woman—with his hands, his mouth.

When he gets home tonight, he'll memorize these names, dream their bodies into being, veins flushed with blood, breath-stretched lungs. He'll kneel with his rosary, his elbows propped on the cushions of his couch, imagining himself at the bottom of that void tank offshore, the sun screaming through the hole in the deck above, and instead of men in paint-splattered coveralls, instead of men with tool belts and filthy mouths and callused hands, he'll see these women descending to him, each of them walking down the ladder without turning her back, without the use of her hands on the rungs, as if this were no less surefooted an endeavor than swishing down a wide, carpeted staircase in a knee-length dress to meet a boy with satin lapels and sweating palms and the intention to press himself, before the night gives itself over to morning, against her.

These women, in his vision, will come to him, come into

the light that shone, Dean knows, more brightly at the bottom of that void tank than it ever did above on deck. They will come and kneel themselves down with him in the metal tank meant to do nothing but hold air, to keep the drilling rig afloat on the ocean while a tugboat tows it from one latitude to the next. And here they will be, kneeling amidst the hot chemical swirl of new paint and urethane sealant he'd been hired, all those years back, to spray, to keep the rust in check, the salt water out. Here, on the hardwoods of his living room floor and in the beaming light that narrows its way into the dark metallic holds of the rig, he will say their names — *Leslie June DeMarco, Jennifer Blue Johnston, Camilla Rosemarie Stump, Bethany Evelyn Green* — and on, and on, until the names become prayers for themselves, until the rosary beads slip through his fingers, one bead at a time — one name, one bread, one body — until their limbs twitch and seize, their musculature turned against them, their eyes rolled backward, looking in. Until at last there comes an immediate release, and sweat drips from them as they blink their vision back into focus and they notice they're kneeling in slicks of paint and pools of light. Until their muscles give them what's left of their bodies back, and they relax, eased at last of the need for what they've surrendered.

In the car, Dean puts his notebook back under the seat, cranks up the a/c against the south Texas heat, rolls his pencil between his thumb and fingers. On the radio, Luanne is paging a new driver, Eighty-two, a heavyset woman with a tiny nose and enormous green eyes. Dean has seen her at the dispatch office only once, when he stopped in one Friday to pick up his paycheck, but drivers come to know each other by voice alone, by the way they joke and complain on the radio. Eighty-two, she's forever running late, calling in for directions, and still Dean finds himself clinging to her voice, wishing he'd never seen her, wanting her body made only of sound. Now she calls in on the radio, her voice an injured trill, so slight that what she says seems spoken only for her own benefit.

"Eighty-two," she says.

"Eighty-two," says Luanne, "I don't know about this, but I've got a run I need STAT, a dedicated roundtrip out to Memorial Hospital in Liberty. You game?"

"Ten-four," the woman says. "Send it across the pager."

Dean shakes his head and does the math. A bankroll run. Three hours, dedicated. A hospital job. Good money. He could drive five hours' worth of local blood and urine samples and still he wouldn't make out as well. He pulls the Velcro straps from his wrist brace and takes the thing off to let his skin breathe. His hand, it's not too bad today. Only the slightest tremor.

Luanne exhales into the handset, her breath crackling over the airwaves. "Eighty-two?" she says.

"Eighty-two, Luanne. Go ahead."

"This job," Luanne says. "This is a fetal demise job. Hospital to downtown pathology. You copy?"

Dean Covin puts his brace back on, pulls the Velcro so

tight it pinches his skin, and if you could be here with him in the car, the air conditioning swirling in your hair while a dead baby's cartage is arranged over the radio, maybe you wouldn't notice that Dean is fiddling with the pencil in his good hand, rolling the thing between his thumb and fingers. Maybe, even if you did, you wouldn't recognize it as the kind of nervous habit that so often begets another. But maybe you would. Maybe you'd touch his shoulder, point to the pencil, remind him about John Dalton, about the eraser swirling in all that gray liquid. Maybe you'd take both of Dean's hands in yours and keep them steady while driver Eighty-two lets the idea of being alone in her car with a cold little body for an hour and a half sink in. Maybe, if you could be here, you'd take that pencil away before Dean Covin lifts it and rests the eraser, out of habit, on his tongue.

But you can't.

The night before his accident, Dean Covin, nineteen years old and stockpiling his offshore cash for a diamond ring, breathed a woman into his lungs. Randi Stimmons, her skin so pale he could see, on nights like this one, when there was moonlight enough, the sweet blue traces of veins in her breasts. Half naked, the both of them, and an hour-long stretch of Highway 288 between this beach and the Houston house where her parents sat in front of the television trying not to watch the clock or listen for the sound of a car finding its late way into the drive, Dean and Randi lay on their backs in the sand, looking up at the racing clouds while the surf slid up to them, slid back, pulling sand from beneath their feet.

And it was agony.

Two years now they'd been grinding against each other. In the sand. On Randi's couch. In Dean's car. Some nights she begged him—*Jesus, baby, just do it*—and the slippery sound of God's name in her throat made it all the worse, made him feel, despite this Texas heat, as if he were frozen under his skin, the ice expanding as his body temperature dropped, cracking him open from the inside out. And still he couldn't bring himself to do it. He would hold her head to his chest and feel himself hardening against her, and her breath would steam through his shirt, through his skin, and yes, sometimes she'd beg, and still he would save himself, but he didn't see it that way. What he imagined was that he was saving her. Keeping her whole, and by doing so, keeping her wholly his. Once, in the car, he'd almost given in, had slipped a finger into her, up to his first knuckle, had felt the tight band of intact tissue squeezing around him. He couldn't help it—it reminded him of a day so many years back, in a restaurant after Mass, when as a child he'd twisted and turned and yanked at his mother's wedding band, trying to pry it from her finger. *It's not supposed to let go*, she'd said. *Not ever.*

But he couldn't tell Randi this. He could barely even admit it to himself. What kind of man—*God, what kind?*—thinks of his mother while his finger is knuckle-deep in another woman? No, instead he'd tell Randi, this night on the beach like so many other nights, that the day would come. That they'd be married and then she'd never keep him off her. That he knew all their other friends were screwing, knew they had been since even freshman year, some of them, but that he didn't want it to be like that, didn't want her to regret it when it happened.

"Fine," she said, sitting up, crossing her arms over her breasts. "But make it soon."

She lit a clove cigarette, blew smoke from her nose, wouldn't look at him.

The truth, he knew even then, was that she terrified him. All that white, moonlit skin. The way he could see through her to the winding of her veins, her body its own blueprint. The way fistfuls of muscles clenched in his back when she put her lips down low near the waistband of his shorts and blew smoke onto his skin. The way he imagined entering her, little by little, in his dreams, until he was burrowed completely into her, living in her body. The way, even just thinking about it, he wondered if he'd lost something of himself that he'd never be able to get back.

And then she did something she'd never done. Taking a drag off her cigarette, she leaned down over him, a hand on his crotch, and kissed him, dipping into him with her tongue, and when he began to inhale, to breathe her in, she blew hard into his mouth and the sweet sting of clove smoke rolled its way down into him.

He sat upright and he held her, her smoke, inside him, until with his eyes wide he saw only the color of blood, a thick and viscous red. When he came to, she was frantic, a constricted face and a moving, voiceless mouth. She leaned over him and a bead of sweat rolled from her armpit down the slope of her side, landed on his stomach. He touched it with his thumb, rubbed it into his skin. He felt her breath, the sharp fire of it, still alive inside him, smoldering, kindling its way aflame.

"Do it again," he said.

They slept on the beach until an hour before sunrise, until the alarm on his watch started beeping. Dean changed into his coveralls and they drove to the Freeport docks so he could catch the crewboat out to the rig. Even with the car windows down, with the sea salt heavy in the air, Dean could smell only Randi. His nose, his sinuses, his throat—they all burned with her, stinging and sweet with cloves. He told her about it, how it felt, like she'd given him a part of herself he could keep inside him, said he hoped it would last the whole two weeks of his hitch. She smiled, shook her head, said, "Not the part I wanted, Dean," and, "You scared the shit out of me."

On the docks, between the overhead barking of gulls and the clomp of his boots on the waterlogged planks, Dean kissed her, said, "Fourteen days," and she stood there while he lugged his duffel to the boat and met up with the rest of the crew at the stern. His boss, Tully, the rig's chief painter, lit a cigarette, put his arm around Dean's shoulders, and waved at Randi as the boat slipped away from the docks. "Boy," he said, "I'm thinking I'd pay upwards of ten dollars just to smell your fingers this morning. I was you I wouldn't make the mistake of washing your hands."

Dean ducked Tully's arm, grabbed his duffel off the deck, said, "What I've got, it doesn't wash off," and stepped down the stairs into the hold to sleep away the hourlong ride to the rig.

Now Eighty-two starts balking. Dean sits in the lab parking lot, lights a cigarette and turns up the two-way, lets her go on awhile about how she doesn't know Liberty all that well, wouldn't want to run late on a job like this, about how she's got only a quarter tank and would have to stop for fuel. He can hear, in the rise of her voice, in the short spurts of static that hiss through his receiver when she squeezes and releases her handset button between sentences, all her real reservations: What do you do, after all, to keep your eyes on the road, to keep your mind on the driving instead of on the cold blue body of your cargo?

These jobs—*fetal demise, dedicated*—aren't all that common, but if you drive medical transport for a few weeks, and if you pay attention to the radio, you're bound to notice how still the airwaves become when a driver announces he's ten-seven from an outlying hospital, the weight of his freight heavier in his mind than it was in his hands as he carried the insulated box from the morgue's walk-in refrigerator to the hospital lobby, through the revolving doors, and out to his car. You can almost hear his relief—he has made it this far, hasn't stumbled, hasn't spilled someone's child onto the worn hospital carpet, the sun-bleached sidewalk—and then, for the next thirty minutes, or an hour, or two, while he's back en route to the city, while he drives past white-flecked fields of cotton or bobbing pump-jacks or the shining pipes of petrochemical plants on his way to the Medical Center downtown, what you notice is the silence, the way the radio chatter is replaced by the whispering hiss of static.

Dean's never run such a job. With a dedicated run, you're either the closest driver to the consigner or you're not, and if you're closest you get the job, assuming you want it. After his morning specimen route, Dean's always standing by at the downtown lab, and these jobs, the ones that make the radios fall quiet, come from small-town hospitals, places without their own pathology units.

Still, whenever he hears a call come through from another driver, one who's ten-seven from some country hospital, one who's no longer quite alone in his car, Dean turns the FM radio off, turns the two-way down. He refrains from smoking. He keeps the windows rolled up and the a/c nice and cool. If Luanne sends a job across his pager, he accelerates slowly and makes smooth, wide turns. He imagines the woman, imagines her outside the hospital, standing from the wheelchair while her husband opens her car door and helps her into the seat, imagines she feels, in that moment on her feet, more off-kilter than she ever did carrying those thirty extra pounds of third-trimester weight. Dean imagines her emptiness, sees a car seat secured on the back seat, the way she catches sight of it as she lowers herself into the car, the way her husband notices her noticing, and the way he's all but gutted by the shame of not having been man enough to see this coming, to spare her yet another injury. He should have had the foresight to pull the thing out of there this morning when he went home to let the dog out, should have stuffed it back in its box, stored it up in the rafters of the garage.

Now Dean puts his cigarette out, rolls his windows up, grabs his handset, and lets Eighty-two off the hook. "Ninety-six, Luanne."

"Ninety-six, go ahead."

"I'll take that dedicated," he says. "I'm heading out now."

There is sunlight on land and there is sunlight at sea, and when Dean stepped from the hold of the crewboat as it rocked and slid in the offshore waves, his eyes still adjusting from sleep, he recognized the difference. In the distance, in every direction, the curved white line of the horizon beamed where the sun found the water and seemed to ignite the surface. The winds held steady and keen, the air thick enough with salt to abrade paint from steel before rust set in; gulls circled above the boat, their beaks downcast, unaware as of yet that they'd followed a boat with no catch, no bait, this far from shore.

Overhead, the rig's crane operator was lowering the taxi to the crewboat deck. It was the kind of ride Dean might have paid a half dollar for at a roadside carnival when he was a kid, a twelve-foot circumference of pipe with a reinforced rubber center, triangles of rope netting strung from the pipe to the hitch above. With four other men, he threw his duffel onto the rubber, stood on the pipe, grabbed tight to the ropes. And up they went, the gulf wind rocking the whole contraption as it rose over the water, up past the rig's lower platform, swinging them over stacks of pipe and safety-yellow handrails to the second deck. The men stepped off, grabbed their duffels, slid five-dollar bills into the binder clip attached to the netting, the crane operator's tip for safe passage, and then, amidst the shouts of the roustabouts and the clanking of pipes, they crossed the deck to the quarters, to the galley, for breakfast before the workday began.

Near noon, his belly still full of steak and eggs, his lungs inflamed even now with Randi's breath, Dean Covin broke a hard sweat in the wet darkness of the void tanks. All morning he and his fellow painter's hand, Gumbo Diggs, had been taking one-hour shifts in the hole. While one man sloshed through the dim cavities of the void tanks, crawling from hold to hold through the portals cut in their steel walls, the other would rest above, monitoring the air compressor and waiting for the tug on the rope that told him the buckets were full, ready to be brought up. So now, while Gumbo smoked in the sunshine on deck and mopped his face with the bandanna he kept tied around his neck, occasionally pulling the plug on Dean's worklight so that everything went black in the tanks—a common enough prank, as was killing the air compressor for a few seconds to stop the flow of fresh air through the hose—Dean soaked through his coveralls and worked a long-pole squeegee down the walls of one of the holds, scraping the old urethane sealant sludge to the floor. When the hold went dark, he cursed Gumbo, imagined him up there in the sunlight, a hulking black man with a shaved scalp and a schoolboy's sense of humor, a man whose mother had taken a first long look at him and named him after a concoction that began with burned flour in a cast-iron skillet. Now Dean waited in a dark so impenetrable that he imagined he could feel his pupils dilating. He wondered if, given enough time, they might expand so that he could actually see down here, see what it was that visited men, unbeknownst to them, in the dark.

Later, when the walls and ceiling were clean, he grabbed the shovel and slopped the thick sludge into a half dozen five-gallon paint buckets. His arms and thighs ablaze with the weight of the work, his lower back stiff from ducking and squeezing through the tight portals, he lugged the buckets one by one back to the main hold, affixed their handles to the rope slung down beside the ladder, and gave the rope a yank.

Above, Gumbo leaned into the sunlight that shot through the deck portal. "Back already?" he said. "What's your hurry this morning? We still getting paid by the hour, ain't we?"

Dean laughed, said he guessed they were.

Gumbo hoisted a full bucket up and gave the rope a little jiggle, raining some of the slop onto the ladder and down onto Dean, who ducked his head to keep the stuff out of his eyes. "Sorry about that," Gumbo said, sending the rope down for another bucket. "Accident."

"Sure," Dean said. "Just make sure you don't accidentally shut the lights off again."

"What the hell, boss. You afraid of the dark now?"

"Of this kind of dark I am."

By the time his hour below was up, Dean Covin had
scraped the holds clean of old sealant. Now, because there
wasn't enough ventilation in the void tanks for sandblast-
ing, they'd have to work with needle guns to chip away
any outcroppings of rust, and then they'd spray new paint
and polyurethane. In a couple days the job would be done,
but the work was endless. Once this network of holds was
finished, Tully would work an impact tool on the flange
bolts of another deck portal and they'd climb down into a
different but wholly familiar labyrinth of dripping sealant
and condensation and a darkness so thick that it too might
as well have been liquid.

When Dean tied the buckets one by one to the rope,
Gumbo hoisted them up, sloshing the sludge over the rims
and raining it down again onto Dean. With the buckets all
up on deck, Dean turned off the worklight, grabbed a rung
of the ladder, and started making his way up, his boots sliding on the wet rungs, his fingers slippery with sweat. Overhead, Gumbo was laughing and the sun came sliding out
from behind a cloud so that Dean found himself climbing
into a loud and blinding light, breathing through his nose,
searching his own body for a trace of Randi's breath.

Two-thirds of the way up, his boot soles lost purchase
and his fingers slipped from their rungs, and when he realized he was falling, when he realized he wasn't dreaming

and the fear flashed hot in his chest, Dean Covin began a prayer he has yet, twelve years later, to finish. *Please, God*—

He hit hard on his back, his head slamming the tank's steel floor. Something sparked at the base of his spine and the world went red before it went black, and when he awoke he found his limbs rigid and twitching, his body no longer his to control. In his ears, a hot humming drowned out all ambient sound, and he couldn't hear Gumbo screaming on deck, calling for Tully, couldn't see anything but blazing white, a light so concentrated and piercing that he could feel its heat beneath his skin, a light so otherworldly that, if you'd been there, maybe up on deck with Gumbo and Tully, peering down into the hold at a man whose body was being racked by seizure, whose eyes were open but glazed and luminous, lit from within, whose apparent demise was spotlighted in such a way that your own body, your head and shoulders, didn't cast a shadow down onto him when you leaned over the portal—if you'd been there, looking down on Dean Covin, you might have dropped to your knees. You might have slid down the ladder to help him. You might have stood, as Gumbo did, momentarily helpless, wringing a sweat-soaked bandanna in your hands while Dean felt the bright touch of this light, felt it as a hand of fingers aflame, each of which were employed now to heat and heal, to cauterize ruptured vessels, to dam the hemorrhaging, to fill him inside with radiance where once there was only body and blood, with a light that seemed as vital now as his own breath, which he noticed was no longer tainted by the taste of salt air or chemical sealants or burning cloves, with a light, he knew even then, that came not from the sun or some high-wattage filament or an adrenaline-triggered flash of his brain's own electricity, but from a flaming hand that lit in him the memory of his mother reading to him, the Bible open on her lap— *And the light shineth in darkness; and the darkness comprehended it not.*

Later, after Gumbo carried him up the ladder on his back, after the life flight helicopter landed and lifted him off to the Medical Center in Houston, after a week in ICU, after the insurance settlements and a year of physical therapy, after Randi told him how sorry she was that this had happened—how it ate her up inside that he wasn't the same man anymore, a man she could love; how she wanted always to be his friend, someone he could talk to—after it all, he called her up one night from the house he'd bought in Deer Park.

"I got a new job," he said. "Caring for the sick." He didn't say how, though he believed it to be true, and he could almost hear her smiling on the other end of the line—a worried, sympathy-laced smile. He told her then that he was getting better, that the seizures weren't coming all that often anymore. He didn't tell her, because he knew it was useless and because it sounded to him more akin to sin than to love, that he'd been wishing, every day since his fall, that he'd been less vigilant on those nights they'd spent together, that he'd allowed himself, if only once, to fill her body with his. No, instead he said, "It was God, Randi. When I fell. He came to me."

"Dean," she said. "Listen. What medicines do they have you on?"

On Highway 90, between the Houston Medical Center and Liberty's Memorial Hospital, Dean keeps his foot heavy on the gas past thirty-some-odd miles of two-pump gas stations, one-room churches with paint-chipped steeples, past rice fields drained and baking beneath the late-summer sun, just days shy of their harvest. When he pulls into the circular drive of the hospital, only fifty minutes into his three-hour deadline, Dean turns on his hazard lights, slides his Gulf Coast Courier credentials onto the dashboard, grabs his clipboard and manifest off the passenger seat, and rubs the thigh of his numb left leg before climbing from the car.

Once inside, he double-checks his pager for the pickup location and rides the elevator up to the third-floor maternity wing, where a nurse with white hair and penciled brows looks up from her charts to find a man incapable of steadying both eyes on her at once, a man whose clipboard is quivering in a braced, crippled-looking hand.

"I'm with Gulf Coast Courier," Dean says, his ears suddenly abuzz with their sourceless humming.

The nurse nods, picks up her telephone and dials an extension. "Poor dear," she says, and Dean can't quite figure if she's speaking of him or of his cargo. "Frank? It's Judy up on three. That driver's here. From Houston."

Before she hangs up, she slides the pathology paperwork toward Dean and signs his manifest. He thanks her, and her clipped smile tells him how unsettling it sounds, to be thanked for this kind of help. "Okay then, Frank. He's on the way down."

In the basement, Dean is met outside the morgue by a towering, slump-bellied security guard holding a Styrofoam box no larger than the ones Dean's father sometimes ships to him around Christmastime from Omaha Steaks. The man shakes his head, says, "I wouldn't want your job today." He hands Dean the box, balances Dean's clipboard atop it, and makes the sign of the cross. "Right this minute," the man says, "I don't much want mine."

Outside the wind has picked up, washing a swollen cluster of clouds over the sun, ripening the air with the smell of cattle and late hay. Dean breathes through his nose as he rests the box against his hip, opening the rear passenger door, and then, thinking twice of it, pulls wide the other door and secures the box on the front seat with the safety belt.

With the engine running and the two-way crackling with static, Dean leafs through the paperwork. At the top of each page, the patient of record is listed as *Whiteside, Sarah Kneeland.* Besides the physician's signature, the only other name on the form isn't a name at all, and something about it—about a child who is no longer a child, who was never quite a child; whose lungs have never held air and whose mother has never held him alive to her breast or called him by name; who is now conspicuously out in the world, boxed up and belted into a strange man's car; whose name, for now, is *Whiteside (Fetal Demise, Male)*—something about it expands cold within him, and he recalls all those nights he'd spent with Randi, how he'd held her off, how she'd tried, with God's name on her lips, to convince him. Now, Dean knows, she's been married and divorced, married again. She's lost to him, except that she so often haunts him, breathing fire into his lungs, dripping sweat onto his skin, and as he puts the car in gear and heads toward Highway 90, the hum in his ears louder than that of his tires on the asphalt, a flash of anger ignites within him the desire to say a rosary for this child's mother, a rosary of imperatives, one that demands rather than begs that her emptiness be filled with something enduring, something solid. Something other than a nameless and bright and fleeting light.

Now he merges onto the highway and, as if to outrun the guilt he feels creeping up already in his wake, he stomps on the gas. For the love of God, isn't he due one day of shortcoming, a day when he can let his anger and self-pity melt away awhile at the chill of his resentments? Here he is, after all, a good man, by damn. A man stricken with purposeless afflictions, with a lazy eye and a bum leg and a nervous tic, with a hand he can't hold steady enough to touch a woman the way a woman wants to be touched.

He checks the speedometer, checks his watch. He'll be back in town in forty-five minutes. There are almost two hours left allocated for his trip, plenty of time for a detour, so when he sets the cruise control at seventy, though he is technically now ten seven from the hospital, he turns the two-way off without calling in. He takes his brace off, lets his hand quake atop the insulated box beside him while he drives, lets himself ask a question he so rarely permits of himself, one that has forever gone unanswered: *How is it, Lord, that you've left me in the world this way?*

The children have vanished. Their bicycle ramp sits abandoned in the street. Dean's noticed this before, how easily, despite their numbers, they can make themselves invisible. Last summer, while fertilizing the front lawn, he'd thought for sure he'd have to make an appointment with his neurologist. The hum in his ears was faint, but there was something else rising in its place. He'd walk awhile behind the spreader, spinning fertilizer onto the grass in front of him, and there it would be, a ghostly, animal chatter, a flittering of wings, but when he turned toward the sound it fell silent. He shook his head hard and went about his work until he noticed a rustling in the leaves of his neighbor's towering pecan tree. He walked closer, and on a thick lower branch beneath a dense overhang of foliage there stood, in a row, six bare little pairs of feet. "Well," he said, smiling, "I'm not going to have a bunch of squirrels making off with Mr. Diggles' pecans when they're still too green to eat. I'd better go get my pellet gun." Then he turned and the children dropped fast and giggling from the tree, scattering in a half dozen directions to hide themselves in houses and hedges.

Now Dean parks in his driveway, straps his brace back, looks up and down the quiet street. He switches the two-way on and calls in. "Ninety-six, Luanne."

"Ninety-six," she says. "Go ahead."

"I'm ten-seven now. Got held up behind a harvester on the way down, but I shouldn't have any trouble getting back on time."

"Ten-four," Luanne says, and then the radio falls strangely silent.

In the living room, Dean puts the box on the couch, throws the front curtains wide to let some light in. He pulls his rosary from its leather pouch on the end table. Then he gets on his knees before this little body in its box.

He crosses himself with the crucifix, thumbs the rosary's medal and recites the Apostles' Creed, an Our Father, three Hail Marys, and then, before he begins the first decade of beads, he lifts the lid from the box. In the car, on the way home, he had imagined this moment, imagined a body swaddled in a new white blanket, its face serene, unexpressive. Here, instead, is something that looks like it's been in the world for an eternity, a body curled into itself, its legs tucked and bent as if arthritic, its skin wrinkled and translucent, tinged with gray.

Dean's bad hand has fallen so still it startles him, and he pinches the next bead hard between his thumb and fingers. He had wanted to replace the prayers of the Sorrowful Mysteries with demands on behalf of this child's mother, to interject her name into every prayer, to kneel until his knees went numb and his body trembled with its own electricity, until he found himself waiting, this baby cradled and shining in his arms, aglow in the hot wash of

light at the foot of the void tank's ladder, until Sarah Kneeland Whiteside descended to him, kissed him softly on the
cheek, and reclaimed her swaddled son.

Instead, when he closes his eyes to pray, when he thumbs
the beads, when the visions come, he sees only himself, a
man with paint-splattered coveralls, a man laid out and unconscious in a deep well of darkness. Helpless.

Dean remembers a promise, a promise of the Virgin that
his mother taught him when he was just a boy, the promise that those who devoted themselves to the rosary would
receive signal graces, and now, now as his hand begins
twitching and his spine tingles with the onset of seizure, he
stands, squeezing the beads in his hand, shaking them hard.

He pulls his cigarettes from his pocket, fires one up,
blows smoke onto the beads. He imagines standing over
that deck portal, pulling the air hose and the worklight up
onto the deck, and what he wants right now is to toss this
rosary inside, to hear it hitting bottom, to bolt the portal
shut and walk away.

And then it comes. The buckling of his legs, the taut
pull of gravity in his chest, the crack of his head against
the hardwoods. The smell of cut grass and rising yeast, of
sweet spices and chimney smoke. The surging release of
his body's energy. He hears chiming, the violent work of
the tongues of bells, and then there is only red giving way
to black.

When he comes to, Dean Covin finds his cigarette burning on the floor a few feet from his face. He tests his legs
and arms, clinches his fists. The rosary is still balled up

in his bad hand. He stands, puts the cigarette between his lips, tucks the beads into his front pocket, and when the chiming starts up again he recognizes it for what it is. Dean takes one last look at this body in its box, replaces the lid. And then he goes to answer the door.

On the front porch, John Dalton stands with his hands out, his palms running with blood. "Check it out," he says. "Pretty nasty, huh?"

Dean's head is throbbing, so he steadies himself with his good hand against the doorjamb. John Dalton's eyes are wet and there's a trickle of snot creeping out of his nose. "What happened?" Dean asks. "What did you do?"

The boy sucks the mucus into his nose, spits into the front hedge. "I bit it," he says. "On my bike. You should've seen it. I totally flew over my handlebars."

Dean nods, looks over his shoulder at the box.

"You gotta help me," the kid says. "I gotta clean this up. My mom sees this, she's gonna freak."

"You bet," Dean says. "Wait here." He heads to the bathroom, grabs a hand towel and a bottle of hydrogen peroxide, and when he comes back out John Dalton is standing in the living room with his eyes on the box.

"What's that?" the boy asks. "What's in it?"

Dean adjusts his brace, pulls the Velcro tighter. He should make something up, he knows. He should fashion a lie the kid will believe, one that will get him away from that box and out of the house, one that will allow Dean to keep him from seeing something a little boy shouldn't ever have to see. Instead there's a flash of his vision, and he sees him-

self flat on his back, a man incapable of summoning comfort, for himself or for anyone else, and now something is
smoldering in him, resignation fanned by curiosity. Why
not? he thinks. Why not stand here and lift that lid, let the
kid have a look, see in the boy's eyes the sudden recognition that he's walking around in a world all too willing to
inflict wounds at random, in a world where even children
stand to lose more than a little skin off their palms.

"It's a baby," Dean says. "A baby's body."

John Dalton looks at the box. Dean expects now that
the boy will challenge him, will refuse to believe what he's
been told, to need the proof only his eyes can give him, but
John Dalton just stares at the box and nods, and when he
looks up at Dean his eyes register only calm acceptance,
then curiosity. "Did you look?" the kid asks.

Dean nods, gravity pulling at him again, but this, he
knows, is not a seizure coming on. No, this is something
different, something he recognizes as the grounding onset
of shame. Here's this boy, after all, bleeding in his neighbor's living room, his eyes wider with fascination and con-
cern than they've ever been when Dean opened a specimen container out on the driveway. What interests the kid,
Dean realizes, what piques his curiosity, is not the body
of a baby packed in Styrofoam on the couch, but the man
standing in front of him, the man he's come to for help. He
wants to know what Dean did or didn't do, to see what kind
of man Dean might or might not be.

Now the boy holds his hands out, says, "I think I dripped
some blood on your floor."

"That's okay," Dean says. "Come on. We'll take care of that on the porch."

Outside, the wounds fizz white when the liquid hits. John Dalton winces but doesn't pull his hands away. Dean dabs at the boy's palms with the towel, pours more of the stuff onto the cuts, and the whole time the kid is talking, talking about the grandfather he lost last year, about how the old man used to take him fishing every summer, about how he looked in his coffin, about how his aunts and uncles kept saying how good the old man looked, how lifelike, how it looked just like he was sleeping. "But it didn't," John Dalton says, spitting into the yard. "His face was all fat. Besides, it was way too quiet. Gramps used to snore his butt off when he slept."

John Dalton blows onto his wounds, shakes his hands a little and nods down at Dean's pocket where part of the rosary is dangling. "Those Mardi Gras beads?"

Dean smiles, tells the boy no, not exactly. "It's a rosary. You pray with it. I was praying."

The boy glances down at Dean's hand, at his brace. "For what?" he asks. "For yourself?"

"For other people mostly. People in need."

The boy holds his hands up, tells Dean thank you, takes a step off the porch, but before Dean can walk inside the boy turns, asks if he's all right. "You don't look so good," he says. "Maybe you should."

"Should what?"

"Say one for yourself. I mean, it can't hurt, right?"

After he shuts the door and checks his watch, Dean

Covin gets back on his knees, because he has time, if he hurries, for one short prayer; because there's a boy out on his driveway who knows already about the permanence of loss, that it can't be concealed, that grandfathers who sleep without snoring can't take you fishing; because Dean knows that the boy is right, knows that in all these years since his accident he's never once said a prayer for himself.

Now he balls the beads up in his bad hand so that he's praying the whole rosary at once, and if you could be there, watching over him, hunkered between the hedges and the house, peering into the front window with a curious little boy beside you, his hands cupped around his eyes while he steams the glass with his breath and smears it with his blood—if you could be there watching while this man inside puts his fist to his moving mouth, you wouldn't hear Dean Covin complete, in a whisper, a prayer twelve years in the making. You wouldn't see what he sees, his body twitching at the bottom of a dark metallic hold some forty miles from shore. You wouldn't feel the light that pours into him and bears him up in such a way that he's floating in midair toward the portal above, rising into the light that will find him, in just a few minutes, not on the deck of a drilling rig, but out on his driveway with an insulated box in his hands, out in a bright world overrun with the likes of Randi Stimmons and John Dalton and Sarah Kneeland Whiteside and Driver Eighty-two and you, all of you aching for what you're walking around without, for what you've lost somewhere along the way to today, the day when Dean Covin walks among you with a limp, and looks at you with a gentle and kind and wandering eye, and shakes your hand with a shaking hand, and knows, despite his injuries, or perhaps because of them, that to be a man, a whole man, is to remain forever in need.

ACKNOWLEDGMENTS

THESE STORIES ORIGINALLY appeared, often in different form, in the following publications, all of whose editors I gratefully acknowledge:

Descant: "Where You Begin"
Five Points: "Something for the Poker Table"
Glimmer Train: "The Only Good Thing I've Heard" &
  "Among the Living Amidst the Trees"
Iron Horse Literary Review: "Monuments"
One Story: "What You're Walking Around Without"
Salt Hill: "An Instance of Fidelity"
Soundings East: "We Don't Talk That Way in Texas"
Story: "Because He Can't Not Remember"
Zoetrope: "The Last One Left in Arkansas"

Many thanks to the good folks at the Sewanee Writers'

Conference, the Ohio Arts Council, Ohio State University, Lone Star College—North Harris, and the Sirenland Writers Conference for their generous support.

A whole passel of readers has helped nudge these stories, over the course of many years, toward their present forms. Special thanks to each and all: Lee K. Abbott, Will Allison, Steve Almond, Stephanie Grant, Michelle Herman, Karl Iagnemma, Marya Labarthe, Mike Lohre, Jason Manganaro, Erin McGraw, Tom Moss, Bryan Narendorf, Dan O'Dair, Kirk Robinson, James Robison, Steve Sansom, Samantha Schnee, Mark Steinwachs, Melanie Rae Thon, Hannah Tinti, Juliet Williams, Tom Williams, Nancy Zafris, and, most especially, Matthew Batt, who reads, bless him, every word I write.

Love and endless appreciation to my parents, my brothers and sister, and to the wondrous and beloved children: Evan, Jillian, and Dalton.

I am forever grateful for my talented, steadfast agent, Irene Skolnick, and for the finest trio of big-hearted women in the publishing business—Adrienne Brodeur, Carla Gray, and Taryn Roeder.

And for the woman who reads, with equal artfulness and care, my sentences and my oft-illegible heart. This is for you, Marya—this and any that may follow.